WILDFLOWER

STEEL CITY SERIES

PIPER LEIGH ION

Published by Piper Leigh Ion

Copyright 2023 © Piper Leigh Ion

Cover Design by Piper Leigh Ion

CONTENTS

To my husband for putting up with my sassy attitude and constant RBF. Whatever it takes.

CHAPTER ONE

"Shit, I'm late. I'm so late." Natalie stuffed her belongings into her bag and scrambled out of the car, slamming the door without a second look. She reached the elevator before it closed, and she broke out into a run the second it opened on her floor. She slid up to the counter of the nurse's station, shooting Melissa an apologetic smile, and pushed her hair back from her eyes.

The head nurse's attention remained on her paperwork. "You're late."

"I know. I'm sorry." Natalie tossed her bag under her arm. "What do you have for me?"

The blonde handed her a stack of metal clipboards. "Those should keep you busy for a while." She tapped the counter with her pen without looking. "The top patient is a Priority One: male, twenty-five years of age, two gunshot wounds and fractured ribs."

Natalie flipped open the file. "Luke Ward. Does he have any family waiting?"

"Yeah," Melissa pointed down the hall. "A group of them, brothers, I think they said, two adult females and two kids."

"Anyone talk to them?"

"Doctor Moore did. Told them it was a sit-and-wait game, and that's what they've been doing."

"How long have they been here?"

Melissa glanced at her watch. "I'd say almost nine hours total."

She shut the folder. "I'm going to throw my stuff into my locker and get started on my runs." She tapped the counter and began walking away, the clipboards tucked firmly under her arm.

"Make sure you clock in first. You're late."

"I know!"

Natalie rewashed her hands and caught her reflection in the mirror. At least she didn't look like she felt. Her shoulder-length hair was pulled back in a tight bun, and her face was light with makeup. Her mother said she didn't need to waste time using it. She learned at an early age that what Mother said was usually what Mother got. Green eyes stared back critically, looking over her full lips and small nose. She wiggled it in distaste, moving away from the sink. She placed the used paper towel into the trashcan and readied the name tag on her blue hospital scrubs.

She nodded in greeting, passing other workers in the hall, smiling occasionally while she slid the folders into each door slot. The large group huddled in the hallway near her last stop. She noticed two kids passed out in the seats. One man spotted her as she approached, and two other men immediately followed.

The first guy was handsome, built with mahogany brown hair brushed back and dark eyes to match. He wore tan boots, dark jeans, and a white shirt under a half-zipped leather jacket. The other two were tall with dark features, one wearing a hat while the other stood before her with a shaved head.

Natalie slid the folder into the slot.

"Can you give us an update? No one will tell us anything."

She shook her head. "I know as much as you do at this point, Sir. He's in stable condition and resting, which I suggest doing yourself."

"We're not leaving him here alone."

"He's not alone, I assure you, but at least get coffee or something to eat. There's a cafeteria on the fourth floor beside the gift shop." She turned towards the door.

"What are you doing?"

"I'm going to check on him."

The man with the shaved head stepped forward. "Can we come in?"

"I'm afraid not. I-"

"That's bullshit," the first man spoke again. "We're his family."

"Mr. Ward-"

"We're all Mr. Ward. We're his brothers."

"Please be patient, and let me do my job. I need to make sure your brother is comfortable. If there are no complications, you can visit him. I am here to help you. Do you understand?"

He stepped back, running both of his hands through his hair. The two other men nodded. "Thank you."

"I'll try to be as quick as possible. In the meantime, visiting the cafeteria or getting some water might be in your best interest. The fountain is located down the hall past the elevators." She gave them a soft smile and stepped inside, shutting the door softly behind her.

Luke Ward looked younger than twenty-six years old. Lying still on the hospital bed, tubes going in and out of his fragile body, he was handsome with brown hair and soft features. He looked so innocent that she couldn't help but feel sympathetic. She always did when it came to patients, even when she didn't know anything about them, sometimes not even their names.

Natalie scolded herself. The man was older than her by two years. He had undoubtedly seen more things than she could imagine. Luke Ward might look innocent, but from the looks of his family, he was anything but.

Moving forward, she checked the machines for his vitals. His heartbeat was strong, the beeping of the machine steady. She gently lowered his wrist back to his side. She exited the room, head down as she shut the door, but the sounds of a heated conversation made her glance up. She caught sight of Dr. Moore as he talked to the three men.

"I understand that you're upset, but-"

"You don't know shit. That's my brother in there, my family, and you won't tell me what is happening. Stop feeding me medical bullshit, and tell it to me straight!"

"Mr. Ward-"

"My name is Martin. You address me by my name. Don't treat me as if I'm just another paying face."

"If you can't control the volume of your voice, Mr. Ward, I will have to ask you to leave."

"Doctor Moore?" Natalie cleared her throat and watched the older man turn towards her. She could have sworn a mixed look of relief and annoyance flashed across his gray-haired features. "Mr. Ward is in steady condition. I don't see where letting his family see him or sit in his room for a while could hurt."

He let out a disgruntled sigh. "I have another operation to attend. Would you be so kind as to explain the necessary precautions, Nurse Hamilton?"

"Of course, Doctor." She waited until he was gone before she focused on Martin. "Sorry about that. We're understaffed due to the cold season, and it can be a bit stressful."

"Doesn't excuse him from being an asshole."

"Sometimes it's best to turn the other cheek, so they say."

He snorted. "Some of us believe that turning the other cheek gets you slapped harder."

"Are you all family?"

"That's Warrick and Anthony. The clinger there is Warrick's girlfriend, Destiny."

Natalie watched in amusement as the woman threw Martin a look of annoyance.

"This is Anthony's wife, Shannon, and their two kids." He shoved his hands in his pockets. "Can we see Luke now?"

"Yes, but he's in a drugged-induced sleep. He lost a lot of blood, and the operation went long due to the gunshot wounds. You were lucky the ambulance reached him when they did, especially in this weather."

"What else is wrong with him? Doc said something about rehabilitation."

"Mr. Ward has fractured ribs and a broken tibia in his right leg. Dr. Moore placed metal pins and adjusted the lining of the bone. He'll have to go through months of physical therapy to regain the use of his leg."

Martin swore under his breath, running his hands through his hair, and she watched him close his eyes.

"From here on out, your brother will need around-the-clock care. He won't be able to do every day things for a while. I can imagine he won't be in the best mood when he wakes up. The medication and staff tend to make even the best quite irritable." She tried to flash a comforting smile. "All that said, your brother is doing well. His vitals are strong and steady. That's an excellent sign."

"How much longer will he have to stay here? We want him home."

"I can't tell you an exact date, but in this situation, you're lucky if he's discharged within a month. That doesn't include outpatient therapy. He'll have to return every week for that." When they nodded, Natalie stepped towards the door. "Come inside. It's okay for the kids to see him too."

The family members thanked her as they walked by, their expressions serious but full of hope. Martin was the last to enter. He stopped directly beside her, his gaze landing on Luke in the hospital bed.

"Thank you for being straight with us."

"I'm doing my job, Mr. Ward."

"Call me Martin." For the first time, he smiled, and it was an expression of honest gratitude. "I appreciate the honesty."

She returned the smile. "You're welcome. If you need anything, there's a call button by the bed and a nurse at the station down the hall. If you have any more questions, don't hesitate to ask for me," she tapped her name tag, "and I'll come as soon as possible."

"Thank you."

With a nod, she shut the door.

It wasn't until six hours later that she took her first break. Natalie sat in the break room and lowered her coffee on the table. She closed her eyes, leaning back against the cold metal, and waited for the hot liquid to cool. Her feet and back ached, but she wouldn't complain. She loved her job. The feeling she was helping people motivated her to keep going. It made her feel useful and needed, things she didn't feel anywhere else.

"You're wasting your time with these people." Her mother's voice echoed through her ears. *"They're below you, Natalie. You should be ashamed."*

Natalie grabbed her cup. She checked the clock on the wall: ten minutes left. She stared down at the liquid and watched steam steadily rise.

"Look at your sister; she's enjoying her life, not gallivanting into some disease-infested hospital with silly fantasies of saving the world. Do you really think you're doing any good? So, you save one person? It doesn't help the millions suffering around the world, does it?" The cold chuckle still echoed through her mind. *"Come home before you embarrass this family more than you already have."*

Four months had passed since she spoke to her mother. She had done a complete one-eighty from what her parents desired, a daughter who threw herself into helping others and being in places most wouldn't have volunteered. She donated her time to homeless shelters, worked at Salvation Army food drives, and helped with the local blood drives.

They were appalled when she applied to a school for nursing instead of business like they wanted. She wasn't interested in their high life of fame and fortune, making money to blow on expensive things and partying all the time. Instead, she turned down offers to join the family business and run one of the largest family-owned corporations in the city. Her father prided himself on providing jobs in the manufacturing of electronic devices and automobiles for what he considered low-income families.

Her sister was sucked into the life of glitter and lies, becoming Mother's perfect carbon copy and doing anything in her power to be more like her as the days passed. She hadn't spoken to Amelia in over a year but imagined the worst for the sweet, pigtail-wearing girl she once knew as her little sister. At times, she wasn't sure who had it worse, herself, who lived daily on her paycheck, or her sister, who would one day find that she was alone, surrounded by money that didn't talk back and give her the advice she desperately needed.

Shaking herself from her thoughts, Natalie finished her coffee and tossed the empty cup into the trashcan. She headed for the outside employee lounge, the electronic doors opening and shutting swiftly behind her.

She spotted the Chief of Medicine sitting alone. Dr. Stewart was nice-looking for a man in his late forties with chiseled solid cheekbones, dark eyes that were always twinkling, and a strong nose that accentuated his face. He had been nice to her since she had taken the job almost seven years ago, quickly becoming the father figure she never had. He was unmarried, and she constantly teased him for spending too much time at the hospital. He always twisted it back around, blaming her lone ranger status on her desire to help patients no matter how busy she was.

Smiling, he waved her over to join him. "Natalie, it's a surprise to see you out here. I didn't know you smoked."

"I don't, Dr. Stewart." She sat down across from him. "I thought some fresh air could do me some good. Why are you out here? I know you don't smoke. You teach annual lectures against it down at the University."

He chuckled and fidgeted with his glasses that rested on the bridge of his nose. "You're correct. I'm on a stake-out."

"Doing what?"

"Catching smokers unaware in their natural habitat."

She couldn't help but laugh. She leaned forward. "I must warn you; they've been known to sway even the strongest protester to the dark side."

His eyebrows rose. "How are things? I noticed you clocked in late today. That's unlike you, Natalie. What does that make it? Your first tardy in three years?"

"It'd be my second tardy in four years," she admitted sheepishly. "My first tardy happened six months after I started third shift when my car broke down."

"Ah, that's right. You're not still driving around that metal form of death on wheels, are you?"

"Thankfully, no. After I graduated nursing school this past summer, I could afford something a little more... Well, a vehicle with doors on it."

They chuckled. He fidgeted again with his glasses. He always did when he was deep in thought or nervous. "You've been here since you were fifteen, Natalie. You've come far from that volunteer candy striper I once knew."

"Thank you. I enjoy working here."

"We're blessed to have someone with such a good heart."

Face flushing, she glowed from the compliment. "Thank you, Doctor." She glanced at her watch. "Well, my break is over. I best get back to my run."

"It was nice to see you again. Take care of yourself."

She stood up from the table. "You too, it was nice to have chatted with you."

"Don't work yourself too hard."

She flashed him another smile over her shoulder. "Same to you. Good luck with your smoker safari hunt."

He let out a deep chuckle, saluting her. She smiled hello as she passed two registered nurses entering the patio area.

"Kim! John! Come have a seat." Dr. Stewart called out. "Still smoking, I see!"

There was panic when she reentered her floor, staff rushing back and forth. She picked up the pace of her steps, eventually breaking into a run past the nurse's station. She skidded to a halt by Luke Ward's room, catching sight of his brothers and family being detained outside while nurses and Dr. Moore hovered around the patient's bed. She signaled to the family she'd be a minute.

Natalie dove into the room, cleaning her hands with disinfectant. "What's going on?"

"Patient is experiencing TC syndrome." Dr. Moore directed the nurses. Luke shook violently on the bed. "I need you to take position by the patient's head, Nurse Hamilton."

She followed directions while the nurses removed all the loose objects from around the bed.

"Let's move him to recovery position on the count of three," he instructed. "One. Two. Three."

They shifted Luke's shaking body on the final count on his injured side. Natalie bent close to his face, checking his mouth to ensure his air passage remained unblocked.

"I need ten ccs of Diazepam!"

A nurse handed Moore a syringe while another tied a tourniquet around Luke's arm. Everyone went quiet as he injected the shot. He handed the empty needle back, and they watched Luke's movements slow, his body relaxing. His chest began to move in and out in a steady rhythm.

"Good work." He took the clipboard handed to him, scribbling down a few notes. "Nurse Hamilton, I will need you to stay on this floor as much as possible. As you're aware, we're running short on staff, so I need you to oversee Mr. Ward in the case of any more emergencies."

"You're giving me clearance to administer?"

He handed the clipboard back to the nurse. "That is, if you think you can handle it. Seven years is enough time to know your way around this hospital blindfolded, don't you think?"

"Yes, Dr. Moore."

"Good." He capped his pen and slid it into his coat front pocket. "You're in charge of this floor until shift change. I will need you to pull a double shift. Are you up to the challenge?"

She wasn't sure, but she nodded anyway.

"Excellent." He made his way out of the room, stopping at the door. "Take care of the family. I have another operation I need to oversee."

Natalie nodded again, and he disappeared into the hall. She glanced around to check that no one was watching and jumped up and down, shaking the tremors out of her hands. As she calmed, she took another look at the patient, checking to make sure that his IV tubes were unrestricted. Satisfied, she flattened her hands over her scrubs and stepped away from the bed.

CHAPTER TWO

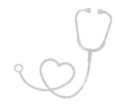

"Is he okay?"

She glanced towards the door and motioned Martin inside. The rest of the family entered behind him, worried looks on their faces. A nurse edged around them, and Natalie recognized her as Reba, a short redhead hired a year ago.

"Is there anything you need me to do, Natalie?"

"He should be fine for another four hours, but please check back in two and oversee changing his IV medication."

Reba nodded, shooting the family a small smile, and excused herself.

"What happened?" Martin demanded. "One minute he was fine, and then...." He directed his attention to Luke. "Should he be on his side like that?"

"Martin, Luke is... May I call him Luke?"

"Of course, he'd hate for anyone to call him Mr. Ward."

"Luke suffered what we call Tonic-Clonic Epilepsy. It's a fancy medical term for convulsions caused by abnormal electrical activity in the brain. Luke simply reacted to the medication. The doctor gave him 10ccs of Diazepam; it's a sedative used to treat anxiety and tension." She glanced towards Luke. "It's common for this type of reaction in patients going through some type of withdrawal. I noticed Luke's hospital records indicated he's a smoker?"

"Yeah," Warrick spoke up. "We've been trying to get him to quit for years."

"I understand. I grew up with a father who always carried an extra cigar in his pocket. When a patient suffers a mild attack and has an injury to the chest, he's placed on the injured side for his strongest lung to assist with fresh air flow. It doesn't harm the injured side."

"Are you saying he has a problem with his lungs now?" Martin questioned, glancing in worry toward his brother. "No one mentioned that."

"Not exactly. According to his papers, a bullet entered the right shoulder between the collarbone bone and right lung. He was lucky because the heart is located near the left lung, so there are no worries of long-term trauma. However, Dr. Moore had to reconstruct parts of the lung. He will recover. The body's internal organs are miraculous for rebuilding themselves quicker than your external given the right atmosphere and time."

There was a knock on the door, and she shifted to see Reba reappear. "Sorry to interrupt, but we've got a UBI that needs your immediate attention, Natalie."

She chuckled at the family's inquisitive expressions. "Unexplained beer injury." She whispered. "Excuse me. Feel free to sit with him now." She followed Reba down the hall, and the nurse motioned her into a room. As soon as she stepped inside, she noticed the lights were out. "Reba, are you sure you..."

Reba clicked the lights on.

"Surprise!"

Natalie covered her mouth with her hand, seeing her friends and coworkers. Dr. Stewart gave her a wave from the side. Her eyes watered at the sight of Nurse Lindsey and Nurse Alice, a decorated cake in their hands with glowing candles as the group began to sing Happy Birthday. Smiling, she blushed and leaned forward to blow out the candles.

"I think I had a heart attack."

"You didn't think we'd forget your birthday, did you?" Dr. Stewart winked. "We may be busier than the day after Thanksgiving, but we don't forget things like that."

"Thank you. I appreciate it more than you know."

He patted her on the back. "Our newest RN deserves nothing but the best."

She stared at him wide-eyed, mouth slack in shock. "Your what?"

"Congratulations, you completed your state licensing examination and on-the-job training." He smiled, slugging her gently on the shoulder on his way out the door. "Don't be late anymore."

"Does the one from today count since it's my birthday?" Her colleagues chuckled, congratulating her and wishing her the best. She thanked each of them with a wide smile. "Would you guys mind putting my cake in the break room for everyone to split?"

"Sure thing, Darling." Alice smiled. "We'll save you the piece with your name on it." She reached for the cake, "You also have a phone call at the desk; it's your mother."

"Thank you." She headed to the nurse's station, biting nervously at her bottom lip. The last conversation with her mother had blown up into a huge argument. She wasn't in the mood for it. She only called to berate her about her career choice or inform her of something fabulous her sister had done. She took the phone from Melissa, clearing her throat. "This is Natalie Hamilton."

"I know who's speaking," Her mother, Veronica, snapped. "Who else do you think I'd be calling at that blasted hospital?"

She leaned against the desk and placed her forehead in the palm of her hand. "Hello, Mother." She rubbed her face in frustration, already feeling a headache approaching. "To what do I owe the pleasure of your call?"

"Don't sass your mother, young lady. I suffered through hours of labor to bring you into this world. You should know better."

She pinched her nose. "I'm sorry, Mother."

"I'm sure you're aware of what day it is." Veronica's voice was smug.

"Of course, it's my-"

"It's not every day your sister gets engaged."

Natalie sucked in air, feeling like she had been sucker-punched in the gut. She squeezed her eyes shut. "No," she choked, "I wasn't aware of that."

"Well, isn't that typical of you, Natalie? Once again, you're too caught up in saving those street rats instead of paying attention to your own family."

"Mother, I haven't spoken to Amelia in a year."

"And whose fault is that?"

"Certainly not mine. I tried numerous times to contact her, and she's too busy chasing after your wants and needs to care."

"Don't you dare talk about your sister that way! Amelia knows her place, and you would do good to take a few pointers from her." Veronica made a sound as if clearing her throat. "She's engaged to a respectful man named Darren Landers; you might have heard of him."

Natalie rolled her eyes. "He's donates money to the hospital and charities around Pittsburgh when he feels neglected by the papers."

"He is the president of one of the largest airlines in this city. I have no idea why he spends his money on such frivolous matters, but what can I say? The man is a charmer."

"More like a snake in the grass," Natalie muttered. She shifted the phone to her other ear as a nurse approached to hand her a clipboard. She flipped it open to scan the contents. "Look, Mother, I hate to cut this stimulating conversation short, but I have runs to make, and I'm already behind."

Her mother let out a disgruntled sigh. "I was calling to extend an invitation to your sister's engagement party tomorrow night, but I suspect you'll be too busy for that, won't you?"

"I'm afraid so." Natalie snapped the folder shut. "I'm scheduled on third shift all week, and a new patient came in today. I'm booked."

"Why can't you get out of it? Your family is more important than some street rat who's there because he got shot stealing a TV or something."

"Your never-ending compassion melts my heart, Mother. I need to go. Please refrain from calling me at the hospital again."

"Natalie Hamilton, do not hang up this phone. We are not done talking!"

"I have to go, Mother." She nodded at the nurse motioning at her. "Congratulate Amelia for me. I would call her, but some of us have to work, even on birthdays." She hung up the phone and rolled her shoulders before glancing at Melissa to find her smirking. "What?"

"I've never heard you talk to your mother with such," she paused as if searching for the right phrasing, "big brass balls before."

Natalie rolled her eyes. "If she calls back, I'm too busy to take her call."

"Is that all I can tell her?"

She shot Melissa a scolding look but smiled. "Yes, thank you."

"Nurse Hamilton?"

Natalie glanced over to see Nurse Rosen still waiting. "Oh yes, sorry, Diane."

"It's okay. I understand." The woman's eyes glanced between her and the phone. "It's the Ward kid. You better take a look at him."

"Excuse me." She slid past Anthony's two children, smiling at them before she handed Nurse Rosen her folders and stepped towards the bed. The family hovered silently near Luke. "What seems to be the problem?"

"It's not exactly a problem, Nurse Hamilton. We changed his medication and placed Mr. Ward in a more comfortable position. It was after that he began to come around."

"He's regaining consciousness?"

Rosen looked disinclined to answer. "His eyes shifted behind the lids, and he whispered a word or two."

"In deep REM sleep, your eyes shift involuntarily. Has anyone tried to establish a physical connection with him?"

"No, I wasn't sure what you'd..."

"No, that's okay." She stepped beside Luke, leaning over him as she slid a small flashlight from her scrubs pocket. "Mr. Ward?" She gently lifted his eyelids, testing with the light for active pupil movement. "Luke, can you hear me?" She glanced down as his lips moved, but no words came out. "Luke, if you can hear me, I need you to respond in any way possible."

She glanced down to see his fingers twitch and turned her attention to his family. "From what I can see, he's reacting positively to the new medication. The spasms have stopped. His pupils are reacting to light stimuli as well. That's a plus when it comes to patients."

"So, he's coming around again?"

"Slowly but surely. It might take a few more days for the medication to take effect."

"Our little brother will be fighting to leave this place soon." Martin grinned over at his brothers. "Luke has never been a big fan of hospitals."

"Most people aren't, Mr. Ward."

"I thought I told you to call me Martin."

"Yeah," Warrick agreed with a nod of his head. "Call us by our first names. We hate that mister crap. Thank you for everything, Natalie."

"Not a problem. I'm just doing my job." She looked at Luke and smiled, brushing a piece of his hair away from his face. Martin noticed the movement but said nothing while watching her closely with a curious look. "Oftentimes, patients in deep unconscious states respond best to physical stimuli. It might be a good idea to talk or touch him."

Martin playfully rolled his eyes. "Luke's fantasies come true. This gets back to him, and I don't know a damn fucking thing about it."

"Man, my kids." Anthony hit him on the back of the head. "Watch yourself."

Natalie chuckled as Martin hit him back without force, and the two little girls giggled. "If you'll excuse me, I need to check on some other patients."

Martin took a seat beside Luke after she left the room. With a smirk, he grabbed Luke's hand with his. "Looks like you got yourself an admirer, Luke. Good thing for you, she's pretty."

Warrick shook his head. "You got a one-track mind, Marty."

"Me? You're the one banging Cruella de Vil every chance you get, and you're fucking loud!"

"My kids, Man! My kids!"

"Your Gomer is in Room Three."

"Thanks, Diane." Natalie entered the room and smiled at the elderly man dressed in a hospital gown. He was perched on the examining table, a deep frown on his face. "Good evening, Mr. Drowser. It's a bit late for you to make a hospital call."

"You're open twenty-four hours a day, ain't cha?"

She chuckled and placed her clipboard on the counter, nodding as she slid the stool over to the table. "For you, Mr. Drowser, always." She put her hands on her knees. "What seems to be the problem this time?"

"Same as the last! I got these dang hives, and they're not going away!"

"I understand, but like I told you the last time, it's due to eating peanut butter. You're suffering from a mild allergic reaction to the nuts."

"But I always eat peanut butter when I watch Wheel of Fortune."

"Perhaps you should try jerky or only jelly?"

"If you say so," he grumbled. "Are you sure it's peanuts? It's not a reaction to some deadly disease or... kidneys? It's a kidney problem?"

Natalie shook her head, covering her laugh with a cough. She leaned over for her pad and slipped a pen from her coat. "Let me write down the name of a doctor. She'll write you a prescription for some ointment. She can give you some more enjoyable substitutions to regular peanut butter."

She slipped from the room to give him a moment to dress and rolled her eyes at Diane laughing by the nurse's station. Gomers were patients who came into the hospital at the first sign of a sniffle. With another chuckle, Natalie made her way back down the hallway.

An hour later, she checked in on the Ward family. Natalie poked her head into the room, smiling at Martin asleep beside Luke, the young man's hand in his. On the opposite side, Warrick sprawled out, snoring in a lounger, head back with his mouth open wide. There was no sight of the rest of the family, and she stepped back into the hallway.

She bumped into someone and turned, recognizing Destiny. "Oh, sorry about that."

"It's okay. You look exhausted. Shouldn't you be resting?" The pretty woman gave her a look of concern, her hands full with two cups of coffee.

"I would, but tick-tock goes the clock." Natalie gestured at the cups. "Coffee for Martin and Warrick? That's sweet of you."

"Not Martin, unless you serve rat poison at this hospital." She smiled at Natalie's surprised expression. "I'm kidding. Yes, they're for my man and the brute."

"I heard that."

They glanced at the doorway to see Martin stretching and rubbing his eyes. "Talking to Destiny will rot your brain. She's like smelling Sharpies for too long. I keep telling Warrick that, but he won't listen."

Destiny scowled, thrusting the cup at him, and Martin looked thankful the cup had a lid. He took a sip and eyed her from his slouched position against the door frame. "Do you ever go home?"

She clutched her folders against her chest. "I'm working a double shift."

"I don't see how you do it, on your feet for hours rushing around helping people. Now, I could do the standing, but all the problems? No, thanks."

"When they start to look like family, you think differently about them." She blushed, brushing away a lock of stray hair from her eyes, seeing his amused expression. "If you'll excuse me, I need to get some coffee."

"Wait, I'll come with you."

Natalie slowed but kept her gaze forward while Martin walked beside her towards the elevators. Stepping inside the car, she punched the number for the cafeteria floor. She glanced out of the corner of her eyes to see him sipping his coffee and leaning against the elevator wall, watching her.

"Something on your mind, Mr. Ward?"

"You seem a little young to take on all this responsibility."

"Age does not denote wisdom."

"I'm not the literary type, Natalie," Martin smirked. "Don't ask me to name the speaker of the quote or anything like that."

She flashed him an amused smile. "It's an old Jewish proverb, Mr. Ward." She stepped out as the elevators dinged open, and he followed.

"How many times do I need to tell you to call me Martin? I haven't been called Mr. Ward since I got a speech from my mother the day they kicked me out of high school." He chuckled at her sideways glance. "I told you I wasn't the literary type."

"What type are you?"

He shrugged as they turned towards the cafeteria. "I'm a simple kind of guy. I take care of my family, and I watch my back. Those are the only two things I worry about these days."

"When you put it like that, you sound more like the complex type of man to me, Martin."

"I hear women usually go for that kind."

"I'm sure you have no trouble with women, despite any side you choose to show them."

"I'm flattered you think of me that way."

She sent him a teasing smile and snatched a cup from the dispenser. She turned towards the coffee machine. "Are you trying to flirt with me?"

"I'd say I was flirting versus trying to, Natalie."

She filled her cup, and taking a lid, she popped back the tiny plastic tab before snapping it into place. "I would say I'm flattered you think of me that way, but I don't usually fall for smooth lines."

"You said usually. Women who say that are open to change in their lives."

"Well, aren't you the expert on women?" She moved away and began to pay the cashier when Martin leaned over, handing the woman money. He smiled, winking at Natalie as he accepted his change and put it into his pocket. She couldn't help but smile back. She shook her head and turned back in the direction of the elevators. "Are you hiding more secrets I should know about? Yodeling maybe? Let me guess, you have a weakness for Hallmark romances."

Martin barked in laughter, a wide grin on his face. "I knew there was a reason I liked you."

"Sarcasm and quick repartee inspire a rise in your sexual levels?" She acted shocked. "I must put a bulletin out and warn the entire hospital staff."

"It might be best to leave it at a beautiful face and intelligent mind."

She was silent until they arrived back on her floor. She sipped her coffee, and when they exited, she looked up at a nurse calling her name. Without another word, she rushed off, leaving him standing there watching her with an amused expression. He cursed as the doors shut on him.

CHAPTER THREE

I f it were possible for limbs to fall off from exhaustion, Natalie was positive she'd be up to her kneecaps with no arms. She glanced at the clock above the nurse's station. At almost nine in the morning, the hospital activity failed to slow down, not that it ever did. She wasn't sure she'd love it the same if it ever were to grow completely quiet. Something about the hustle and bustle made her come alive.

Sighing, she picked up a folder and headed to the nearest waiting patient. She was taking a blood sample from a patient when there was a tap on the door. "Just a minute."

"Natalie?"

She looked over to the door. "Dr. Stewart, what can I do for you?"

He smiled comfortingly at the patient, a young boy of twelve, and nudged his head at the hallway. "When you get a moment, your mother is here to see you."

Her back stiffened. She bit her bottom lip and finished her sample as gently as possible. She held down the cotton ball, handed the syringe to a waiting nurse, and placed a band-aid over the ball. Natalie bent the boy's arm up towards his chest. "Hold your arm like that, Timmy. It'll help stop the blood flow. You can lower it back down in one minute, okay?"

"Okay."

She patted him on the shoulder. "You did a great job." Collecting her papers, she stepped out of the room with Dr. Stewart and allowed him to pull her toward a sheltered part of the hallway. "I don't think I can handle her right now, Dr. Stewart."

"I'm afraid you have no choice, Natalie. She's been on every floor demanding to speak to you and said she's not leaving until she does. She brought a slightly large fellow, a bodyguard or something."

She let out a dry chuckle. "That'd be Bruno. Trust me, he's like a big puppy dog. He follows her everywhere for show. I'll get rid of her soon, don't worry."

"I'm not worried about her. I'm worried about you." Dr. Stewart shook his head. "You've been here for twelve hours straight. If you continue to push yourself, I'm afraid you might burn yourself out, and I don't mean in a calm, recharge way."

"I understand what you mean. You don't have to explain it to me by connecting the dots. I'll be fine."

"I mean it, don't overexert yourself. You're too important to us to lose due to a bad judgment call." He shook his finger at her. "I'll watch your patients while you take a break and talk to her. If you need me, call."

"Thanks, Dr. Stewart."

He rolled his eyes. "You'd think by now you'd call me Thomas."

"You'd think." She flashed him a smile and approached the nurse's station. She could already smell her mother's intense perfume. Had she mastered invisibility along with the ability to repel all things human?

Natalie stiffened her shoulders, raising her chin as she came up behind her mother and watched as Bruno pointed, muttering something to the woman he towered over. Her mother turned; her dark red lips compressed together in a flat line of annoyance.

"I have been all over this damn hospital looking for you!"

Veronica Hamilton had once been a beautiful, vibrant woman, but endless smoking, drinking, and an evil heart tainted her. She was tall, almost five foot nine, with long dark black hair and flashing green eyes. Years of the best cosmetic surgery and enhancement had made her skin marble. Her lips were usually pressed flat, a straight line of disgust evident, but whenever she smiled, it always made Natalie shiver, the look predatory and snakelike. She was the snake that always smiled right before she ate her prey.

"What can I do for you, Mother?"

"I told you not to hang up on me. Now, I've had to drag myself down to this..." Veronica glanced around, shifting the fur scarf closer around her neck, "wretched place. I'll simply have no choice but to take another bath to get the stink off me."

"Why are you here?"

"I'm here to take you home. There's simply no reason you should be here any longer. Amelia will be delighted you've decided to attend her engagement party. You'll buy something nice to wear and a gift before we go."

"I already told you I can't attend her party, Mother. There's no way I'm leaving the hospital. I have patients. I can't leave them."

"And why not? It's not like it's any concern to you when they die."

Natalie flinched as several nurses glanced up at the station, Melissa hovering over the phone. "I'd be most appreciative if you never said anything like that again."

"Or what, Natalie? You're still a child. Don't you dare try to order me around! I am your mother!"

"Well, you're not my mother." Melissa hissed as she stood up from her desk chair. "If you can't control your emotions, Ma'am, I will have someone escort you out."

Bruno made a grunting noise, but Melissa refused to sit back down. She lifted the phone, and Veronica rolled her eyes before focusing back on Natalie.

"See? You hang with such low-status people, Natalie. It's dragging you down and turning you against me. I've done a lot for you, bringing you into this world and making you into the woman you are today. This is the thanks I get?"

"Don't be ridiculous," Natalie exploded. "I had a nanny from the day I was born until I moved off to college." She narrowed her eyes, the wave of confidence coming off Melissa and those around her giving her strength. "Patricia was the only mother I knew growing up. She was the only one who ever gave a damn about me. Don't you ever dishonor her memory like that again!"

"Natalie, you will-"

"I think it's time you leave."

Veronica's mouth dropped open as she stared at her. "You better think wisely about your choices, Dear," she hissed. "If you ever want to show your face in this town again with any sort of dignity, you'll stop this nonsense this instant and come with me."

"I think she said she wanted you to leave."

Her eyes flashed angrily over Natalie's shoulder, narrowing as they landed on the man who spoke. "And what concern is it of yours?"

"I'm her boyfriend," Martin stated firmly as he stood beside Natalie, "and I don't take too kindly to people harassing my girlfriend."

Veronica gazed between them, an amused look appearing on her face. "When I thought you couldn't sink any lower, you've found a street rat of our own. No wonder you're afraid to come home and show your face." She smirked at Martin. "Let me guess, you got her pregnant, and now she has no choice but to support the both of you?"

"That's enough," Natalie spat. "If you insult Martin one more time, I'll throw you out of here myself. He's a wonderful man, and he's definitely a better man than your horrible excuse for a husband will ever be." She slipped her hand into Martin's, holding back her surprise when she felt him squeeze her fingers in a supportive motion. "I think you know the direction of the exit."

Veronica snorted but threw the scarf over her shoulder again dismissively. She flicked her fingers at Bruno. "Let's go. The contaminated air in this place is beginning to dry out my hair." She leaned forward. "Don't think about trying to crawl back to us when this falls apart, Natalie. From this point on, you don't have a family anymore."

"That's where you're wrong." She met her mother's gaze. "The only family I need is right here." She remained standing where she was until the elevator doors slid shut behind Veronica and Bruno. The tension immediately slipped out of her, and she let out a rush of air, blushing as the staff around her began to clap. Melissa shot her a thumbs up as she sat back down. She glanced down at her hand still in Martin's.

"Oh, sorry." He grinned and pulled away.

She blushed again. "I guess I should thank you. No one's ever stood up to my mother like that before."

"From the looks of it, that included you."

"Afraid so." She glanced past him to see Dr. Stewart and waved with two fingers. He returned to the signal before he disappeared into the elevator. "My boyfriend, huh? That's certainly news to me."

"It was to your mother, too." Martin laughed. "I enjoyed that part the most. Well, second behind you telling her where she could stick it."

"I don't know what came over me. That wasn't me." Natalie shook her head. "I've never been that rude. I don't like how it makes me feel."

"There's nothing wrong with standing up for yourself, Natalie. If you don't do it, no one else will."

"You and Melissa helped me..."

"You stood up to her first. Remember that."

She managed to smile. "How is your brother doing? I was about to check on him, but since things his way were quiet, I figured Reba had him covered." Martin studied her, and it made her fidget. "What?"

"After what happened, you still have your mind on someone other than yourself."

"It's my-"

"Job, I know. Luke's fine, and Warrick's with him. We've decided to stay with him on rotating shifts until he gets better."

"You plan on doing that for almost a month?"

"It won't take Luke long to recover. Trust me, he's a Ward."

Natalie shifted her folders in her arms. "I hope you're right, Martin. Luke has a long road ahead of him. So far, despite the bumps, he's doing excellently."

"Like I said, he's a Ward."

She began to say something else when she spotted Reba from the corner of her eye. "Yes, Reba?"

"It's time for your last break."

"No, I took one to..."

"That wasn't a break." Reba took the papers and folders despite her protests. "Dr. Stewart says you're due to end your double in a few hours anyway, so you're to clock out now."

"But I-"

"Your next shift is at 10 o'clock on Friday. He instructed you to use your day off wisely." Reba pivoted on her heels, a smile on her face as she left her standing there empty-handed.

Fatigue suddenly caught up with her, making her too tired to argue. "Fine, you guys win."

"Go home," Melissa muttered. "Go rest those big brass ones. I bet they're sore from all the beatings they gave today."

"Melissa!"

The nurses laughed as they began to work again, the phones ringing and papers exchanging.

"Come on," Martin nudged his head. "I'm headed home. I'll give you a ride."

"Thanks, but I drove here."

"Damn, a golden opportunity missed."

"Thank you again for what you did."

He shrugged nonchalantly. "It was nothing. You're taking care of my baby brother. I'd do it again in a heartbeat. My family owes you. We won't forget your kindness."

"I wish nothing more than a speedy recovery for your brother."

"Me too," Martin whispered as she disappeared towards the employee lounge. "Me too."

Natalie stepped out of her warm apartment and into the cool morning air. Steam was coming off her breath as she placed her feet wide on the concrete and reached down to touch her toes. She came back up and raised her arms over her head.

"If I were young again, I'd still be asleep."

She grinned over at her neighbor, an elderly woman who had lived there long before she moved into the apartment complex. "What are you doing out so early, Mrs. Thompson?"

"Grocery shopping." The woman smiled and lifted the two bags in her hands. "They had a sale on tomatoes and rutabagas down at the market. I couldn't help myself."

Natalie quickly hopped down the steps, moving to take one of the bags. "Here, let me help you."

"Thank you, Ms. Natalie. You sure are a sweet woman."

She smiled her thanks and followed Mrs. Thompson up the steps. "How have you been? Gone on any dates lately?"

"Me? Dates?" Mrs. Thompson giggled. "Heavens, no!"

"Attractive woman like you, surely men are banging down the door."

Mrs. Thompson opened her door and motioned for Natalie to follow. "I think I should be asking that. Girl like you should be going on dates, not always working. Any men in your life? You know I love the gossip."

She placed the paper bag down on the kitchen counter. "Hospital life doesn't leave much room for dating."

The elderly woman gave her a scolding look and patted her shoulder. "Don't spend the rest of your life alone because you fear it might not work out. I never would have met Mr. Thompson, God rest his soul, if I hadn't gone out and caught him."

"I'll keep that in mind. I hate to disappear on you, but I never will if I don't go running now."

"Young people and the need to exercise when you're already thin." Mrs. Thompson shook her head, following Natalie back to the door. "I'll never understand it."

"I think it is something that still puzzles us as well." She bound down the steps. "Have a great day, Mrs. Thompson."

"You too, Sweetheart. Be careful out there. Remember what I said!"

Waving, Natalie jogged down the sidewalk. She pressed play on the playlist on her phone, putting in her earbuds right when an energizing pop song flooded her ears. She ran around the block several times before she turned off her music, breathing hard as she wiped the sweat from her forehead and climbed the steps to her apartment. She paused, hearing a cough, and looked up wide-eyed to see Martin Ward leaning against the wall beside her door.

CHAPTER FOUR

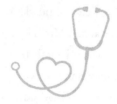

Dressed in boots and dark jeans, the jacket now familiar, the sight of a gray sweater sticking from beneath it informed her he must have left the hospital with enough time to return home to shower.

"Mr...." she paused, "Martin, this is a pleasant surprise."

"I'm glad to hear it. I wasn't sure how you'd react to me showing up, but I thought I'd take my chances."

"How'd you-"

"Melissa gave me your address." Martin bent down, lifting two plastic bags in his hand. "I brought you some lunch."

Natalie fished her key out of her sock, ignoring his amused look, and smiled. "That's nice of you." She glanced towards Mrs. Thompson's door. "Come in, please." She shut the door after him, clearing her throat as she placed her house key on the rack by the door. "What do I owe the honor of you buying me lunch?"

Martin shrugged and looked around her apartment. He flashed her a smile as she took one of the bags. "I figure you might be one of those people that likes to eat lunch around noon," He chuckled when she blushed, "and partly, I thought it'd be a nice extra little thank you."

"Martin, you don't have to keep thanking me. Dr. Moore is the one who saved your brother's life, not me." She kept her gaze down, concentrating on fetching plates and silverware, aware that he followed her into the kitchen close behind her. "I'm merely the nurse who ensures your brother rests comfortably. There's really no need to feel obligated to..."

"I said partly," he interrupted. "I'm going to be selfish and admit I wanted to have lunch with you. I couldn't think of a better excuse."

She turned away to grab two cups, blushing so hard she swore she felt it to her toes. Martin was a handsome man, devoted to his family, and he knew how to choose his words regarding women and what they wanted to hear. The thought made her pause.

Sophomore year in college, Eric Williams had known from day one what words to say. All he had done was throw her that winning smile, and she accepted anything he said without hesitation. She had spent two years trying to keep him happy, and it still had blown up in her face. They were too different, their goals too distant, and they had no connection. She was heartbroken when he took a job in San Francisco, breaking up with her the day he left. Natalie vowed never to get involved with another man again. She chose to concentrate on what she did best: helping others.

She stuck by that plan for years, yet she invited a patient's brother into her home.

"Is everything okay?"

Natalie cleared her throat and watched the ice machine fill the glasses. "I'm fine, thank you." She turned towards him. "What can I get you to drink?"

"You wouldn't happen to have beer, would you?"

"It's nine forty-five in the morning, Martin."

He chuckled. "Water is fine."

Smiling, she turned back to the fridge with a shake of her head. "I don't have any beer, so you'd be out of luck anyway."

"Ah, not a fan?"

She filled both glasses with water and turned to hand him a glass. She motioned him to sit at the kitchen table. "I'm not a huge fan of drinking. I see too many cases at the hospital that ended in tragedy to get near the stuff." She giggled at the expression on his face. "Oh no, I've insulted a whiskey man, right?"

Martin grinned, taking the plate she extended towards him as he grabbed a knife and fork. "No offense taken, trust me, but I enjoy beer and occasionally, something harder every once in a while."

Natalie slid the to-go boxes from the bags, placing them on the table between them. "And you're not worried about a beer gut?"

"My body's in good condition. You're a nurse. I bet you'd approve. Got a hospital gown lying around here?"

She went still until she realized he was teasing her. She blushed and reached to open the boxes. "Sorry, my imaginary boyfriend took my last one and won't return my calls so I can get it back."

Martin laughed, watching as she caught sight of the Chinese food and inhaled, a small smile on her face.

"I love Chinese food."

"I know. I asked Melissa."

She rolled her eyes playfully, making a mental note to talk to Melissa the second she returned to work. "Good thing you did. I would have kicked you out if you'd brought me something I didn't like," She teased.

"Kick me out? I'm too charming for that."

Too strong, she wanted to say, but she chuckled as they began to eat. She had seen the look of anger in his eyes when he talked with Dr. Moore. Inside Martin Ward, there was a distraught man. Natalie swallowed a piece of sesame chicken and chased it down with a sip of water. "How is your brother doing?"

"Great. Dr. Stewart said he's improved a lot on the new medication. They're hoping he'll be awake by the end of next week."

"That's excellent news. Your brother is a strong man."

"Little Brother has some fight in him, all right. A Ward, through and through. I won't be surprised if he's awake and talking by Tuesday morning."

She took another sip of her water. "I'm pleasantly surprised to see Dr. Stewart has taken such an interest in your brother. He's usually too busy to even come down to our floor, you know how bigwigs are."

"I think he's curious. Luke's doing a lot better than anyone expected. I mean, shit, I didn't expect him to make it this far. I thought I'd lost him..." He tightened his grip on his fork, staring off into space.

"What happened?"

He directed his gaze at his plate, stabbing a piece of chicken with his fork. "He happened to be at the wrong place at the wrong time."

"Was it gang-related? I mean, you could go to the police and..."

"I'd really prefer not to talk about it." He fixed her with a hard gaze. "It's hard enough as it is with having to remember it in my head."

Natalie nodded, reaching out to place her hand on his arm. "It's okay, Martin. You don't have to tell me anything you don't want." She was silent for a few moments before she chose to speak again. "You're not weak if you want to discuss it with a professional."

He removed his arm from under her hand, scooting the chair back. "I don't need a fucking head doctor."

"I didn't mean to imply that you..."

"You know, maybe this was a bad idea." Martin wiped his mouth. "I shouldn't be doing this. I should be at the hospital next to Luke, where I belong."

Natalie stood at the same time, and she reached out, grabbing his arm when he turned towards the door. "Wait, please."

His body was stiff, but he allowed her to tug him so that she could see the side of his face.

"I'm sorry. I didn't mean to overstep my boundaries." She bit her bottom lip. All the training in the world never prepared a person to deal with someone who had almost suffered the loss he had. "Luke wouldn't want you to torment yourself this way. He's doing fine. He won't hold it against you if you enjoy eating lunch, though he might get annoyed you're doing it with his nurse."

"Eating lunch, you mean?"

Natalie laughed and pulled away, motioning back at the table. "Stay for lunch. You can go to the hospital and see him as soon as you're done."

Martin moved back to the table. "I'm sorry I blew up. You're only trying to help."

"It's perfectly fine." She sat back down and picked up her fork again. "So, what's your brother like when he's conscious?"

He laughed and joined her at the table, scooting forward as he began to tell her about his family.

It wasn't until an hour and a half later that they finished their meal and washed the dishes. She was surprised when he insisted on helping her, but it gave her more time to ask questions about himself and his family while he dried the wet items.

As expected, his adopted life was filled with happiness and love. Eleanor Ward was an extraordinary woman by the sounds of it, taking in two lost kids and making them honorable, respectable men who knew the true meaning of love and family. It was at that moment she no longer felt utterly sympathetic towards Martin. Instead, she was filled with envy.

"What happened to your mother?" She put the last dish away and turned to gaze at him. "I mean, I'm sorry. I shouldn't have asked that. You don't have to answer."

He cleared his throat. "She passed away about a month ago. She was mugged and shot on her way home from the grocery store. She didn't make it."

"I'm so sorry, Martin."

"It's okay. I fought my demons, and I'm at peace with it now."

"Well, at least you fought them and won. That's always a step forward."

"I couldn't agree with you more. I'm surprised you didn't hear on the news."

Natalie shrugged nervously. "I don't have cable. I don't have time to keep up with current events with how much I'm at the hospital."

Martin glanced down at his watch. "Speaking of the hospital, I better get going. Luke's probably missing me by now."

She smiled and followed him to the front door. "Thank you for lunch. It was a pleasure to talk to you. I appreciate you sharing your family stories with me. It's not often I get to know the patient personally that I'm caring for these days."

"I enjoyed myself, too. Thanks for everything."

Natalie rested her hand on the doorknob. She swung open the door. "Hope everything's well with Luke at the hospital. I'll be back in tomorrow at ten to check on him."

"Thanks again, Natalie." Martin hesitated only a second before he leaned forward, his hand finding her shoulder. He brushed his lips lightly against her cheek. "See you later."

"Bye." She whispered, watching him bound down the steps toward his car. She stood there until he disappeared down the street in his car. A cough caused her to jump, and she tilted her head to see Mrs. Thompson on her porch, the woman sipping lemonade as she stared at the paper in her lap. She glanced up to catch Natalie's gaze and winked before focusing back on her article of interest.

Chuckling, she shut the door and leaned back against the wood with a sigh.

"Natalie, I'm so glad that you're here."

Eyebrows up, she stared at Reba in confusion. "Why? What's up?"

"Four new patients came in this last past hour. I took care of one already, and Dr. Moore is in surgery right this second." She handed Natalie four metal folders, pointing to the one on top. "I left an Appy patient and a tough stick that you might want to look at."

Natalie flipped open the first file. "An Appy? Why didn't you send him to the third floor? They handle appendicitis patients down there like common colds."

"I can do that right away."

"Thanks. Also, give Diane the tough stick. She's good at drawing blood like a vamp."

Reba nodded again and took both files.

"Where's Dr. Masser? Wasn't he supposed to be on this floor starting tonight?"

"He called out today." Reba shrugged. "Guess he's still in Aspen with his family. Dr. Moore said he's leaving in twenty minutes, so I guess that leaves you with the floor again."

Natalie bit the inside of her mouth. "Alright. What patient is he with now?"

"A Virgin Abdominal. He's about done. It's the last folder."

"Thank you, Reba. You did an excellent job. I appreciate it."

"Sure thing. Anything else I can do for you?"

"No, I'm good. Go take a break."

"I'm not going to argue with that."

Natalie turned towards the station and smiled at Melissa. "How's the Ward kid?"

"Kid? He's older than you."

She rolled her eyes playfully. "I'm aware. Come on, what's the 411?"

"He's fine, still hasn't woken up. Members of his family have been here off and on. They're doing this-"

"Shift schedule," Natalie nodded. "Yeah, Martin told me."

"Oh, your boyfriend."

"He's not my boyfriend."

Melissa began to whistle under her breath with a smile. "Whatever you say, Honey."

"He's not!"

"Fine-looking man like that could be my boyfriend any day of the week." Nurse Cook spoke up from behind Melissa. She turned from putting sheets into a mailbox to wink at Natalie. "Or night, for that matter."

"You want him so bad; you can have him. He's not my boyfriend." Natalie scooped up the folders, thrusting them under her arm. "And I'd appreciate if you'd not speak that way about a patient's brother again."

Nurse Cook and Melissa watched her march off, and they nodded at each other.

"He's her boyfriend."

Only the lamp on the overhead above Luke's bed gave light to the room. The steady beeping of machines was the only sound that met her ears apart from his soft breathing. She was surprised to find him alone.

Natalie approached the bed, pulling a chair close to it. She cleared her throat and reached out to take his hand. "Hi, Luke. You don't remember me. It was a bit crazy the other day when we first met; it always is," she giggled. "I'm Natalie. I'll be taking care of you." She placed her other hand on top of his. "Your family is here, and they need you to get better as soon as possible, especially your brother, Martin. He sure does love to tease you a lot, but he loves you very much." She kept her gaze on his face, watching his eyes occasionally shift behind his eyelids. "I bet you're dreaming right now. That's okay," she stroked his hand, "but sooner than later, we're going to need you to come back to us."

"Martin says he seems to respond the most when you insult him."

She twisted in the seat, lowering Luke's hand back to his side, and stood as Warrick entered the room. He slid his hands into his coat pockets and glanced at Luke on the bed.

"But I've never listened to Martin's ideas before, and I'm not going to start now."

She cleared her throat, nervously placing her hands behind her back. "I'm sorry. He was alone, so I thought I'd..."

"It's perfectly fine," Warrick smiled. "Luke won't complain about a pretty girl holding his hand."

Natalie smiled back. "I'm glad to see he's better."

"Dr. Stewart said if he kept up this recovery speed, he'd be walking around in no time."

"We can all hope. Are you starting your shift now?"

"It looks like it's me for the night. Martin will swing by when he gets off work. Tony is doing something with his family, and Destiny's mother is in town visiting from Arizona."

"Well, if all stays quiet, I can help you."

"That'd be great, thanks."

Natalie glanced once more at Luke and offered Warrick her seat. "I'm going to check on some other patients. I'll be back shortly."

Shortly turned into four hours. Natalie smiled, waving at a patient headed to check out, and she spotted Reba approaching her. "Please. Do not say, 'one more patient' to me."

Reba shook her head. "You're good as gold, Nat. We've slowed down, and it's only two. The second floor sent us some extra help. It seems they had more come in tonight than they thought they sched-uled."

"Good. I'm going to take my lunch. Page me if you need me. If not, I'll find you again in about an hour."

"Sure thing, Nat."

She walked away, heading automatically for Luke's room, and leaned in, tapping on the door frame.

Warrick looked up and stood, stretching his arms. "Hey, Doc."

"I'm not a doctor, Warrick."

"The way I see it, you're Luke's doctor. You've cared for him more than any soul in this hospital." He popped his neck, checking his watch. "Do you mind if I run to the house and check on Destiny? She's not answering the phone, so she either forgot to hang it up or..."

"No, go ahead. I'm on lunch, so take your time."

"Are you sure? I could wait till you get some food."

"I'm okay." Natalie ushered him towards the door. "Be careful. The roads are slick."

He stopped halfway outside the door. "Thanks, Natalie."

"You're welcome."

She took his seat beside the bed and shifted it so she could rest her feet harmlessly on the edge. She reached over to take his hand and thread her fingers through his. He remained asleep. "Do you know how hard it is to hold hands with a guy that won't squeeze his fingers?" She chuckled, watching his face. "I bet you'd freak out if you woke up right now. You don't look like the kind of guy that holds hands with a girl when he doesn't know her name." She tilted her head. "I could be wrong."

She leaned her head back, staring briefly at the ceiling. "I wish I knew what happened to you, Luke, but your brother seems adamant about not talking. None of your brothers have," She glanced over at him again, "but I bet you'd tell me, wouldn't you?" She leaned forward, kicking her feet off the bed, and reached over to brush away a piece of his hair from his forehead. "That's twice I've done that now," Natalie murmured. "A girl could get used to that kind of thing."

She tilted her head as she continued to study his features. "I bet you have a girlfriend no one knows about, or maybe you have a hobby like painting." She smiled slowly, "I bet you're in a band. Are you in a band?" Natalie studied his fingers. "Definitely in a band with these fingers. Do you play the guitar, Luke?"

She began to lean back when she felt a spasm against her thumb. She frowned, ceasing her movements to inch even closer to him. Her eyes were drawn to his hand clasped in hers. She watched, eyes wide, when his fingers twitched again and curled around hers.

"Luke?" Natalie stood up from the seat, shoving it back using her foot. Blindly, she reached for his call button and squeezed the red trigger. She tossed it aside. "Luke, can you hear me?"

A wide grin spread across her face the second he squeezed her hand.

"That's right. Come back to us." She sat on the edge, careful not to crush his tubes or touch his side. She squeezed his hand back. "Come back to me, Luke. You can do it."

"Nurse Hamilton, we saw the light." Reba burst into the room with Diane following close behind her. "Is everything okay?"

His eyes opened at that exact moment, his mouth moving soundlessly.

Natalie grinned down at him. "Welcome back, Mr. Ward."

CHAPTER FIVE

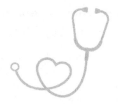

Martin jogged out of the elevator, Anthony following close behind with Destiny, and they ran up to Warrick standing outside the door of Luke's room.

"What's going on?"

"He's awake?"

"Why aren't you in there?"

"Whoa, one question at a time." Warrick waved his hands. "Dr. Stewart is in there right now with Natalie. We can't go in there until they're done."

Martin ran his hands through his hair with worry still on his face. "What happened? Were you here?"

"I was going to the house when I remembered I forgot my keys. I returned, and all these people were going in and out of his room. Natalie told me Luke woke up." A big grin appeared on Warrick's face as he hugged Destiny. "She was talking to him, and he woke up!"

Eyes on the door, Martin stepped forward.

She greeted the group with a smile. "He's doing fine."

"Fine? Just fine?" Martin pressed. "Come on, Nat, tell us more than that! Please!"

"I'll let Dr. Stewart handle that part."

Dr. Stewart slipped out of the room and tucked his small flashlight into his front lab coat pocket. "Let me start by saying that a case such as your brother exemplifies is extremely rare. Possibly, one in a million patients each year experience it. Thanks to a change in IV medication and quick thinking by Nurse Hamilton, Mr. Ward responded very strongly. Due to physical connection and voice recognition, he was able to come out of his coma earlier than we expected."

Martin frowned. "Voice recognition? We weren't here."

"No," Warrick agreed, "We weren't." His eyes went to Natalie.

"Nurse Hamilton has been on close calls with Mr. Ward more than any of us. He responded to her first. This doesn't mean he didn't benefit from your time with him, but like I said, this type of situation is highly unusual. I believe there is no explanation that would satisfy you all and our medical board."

"Can we see him now?"

"Of course," Natalie nodded. "He's been asking for all of you." She ushered them inside and hung back, watching each brother greet Luke with a smile. He smiled weakly at them as they circled the bed, patting him on the arms or legs.

Natalie began to shut the door, and her gaze caught Martin's. He smiled, nodding at her, and she returned the gesture before the door separated them.

"Luke, Baby Brother! About time your lazy ass got up!"

"You are a sight for sore eyes, Sweetheart!"

"Glad to see you back, Luke."

He glanced around at them, smiling weakly. "Hey."

"You want some water, Man?" Martin moved forward, grabbed the cup off the tray by his bed, and extended it towards Luke, tilting the straw for him. "Got it ready for you."

Luke sipped for several seconds before he leaned back against his pillows. "Thanks."

Martin set the cup back down. "Gotcha covered, Little Brother, but don't think this hand and food shit will last forever. As soon as you get on your feet, it's back to being our chief."

They all chuckled, exchanging happy smiles.

"How do you feel?" Anthony questioned. "Are you still woozy from the medication, or do you feel like you could walk around?" He glanced up to find them looking at him strangely. "I didn't say for him to do it! I asked if he felt he could! Geez."

Luke licked his dry lips. "I'm a bit dizzy. I ache everywhere. The pain that comes and goes."

"We're going to hook you up with the best medicine." Martin patted him on the arm. "You'll be so high you won't come down for years."

Warrick nodded. "As soon as you're better, we're out of here."

"That's right, Luke. We'll get you home, and you can sit around and order Destiny to make you all the meals you want."

"I'm good at making ones, except for Martin's that I spit in first."

He shot her a look, and she smiled innocently, causing Luke to laugh. He coughed but shook his head as Martin reached for the water again. "I'm okay." He managed to smile. "I see I haven't missed much."

"Nah, she's the same ol' pain in the ass. Do you want us to leave you alone? I mean, I doubt you want to sleep, but..."

"I am tired. I feel like I've been trapped inside my head for days, hearing this voice I didn't recognize." Luke eyed Martin. "She kept telling me to come back, but I don't know who she is." He paused. "Maybe I'm going crazy."

"You're not any crazier than the rest of us." Martin smiled. "Did you talk to Natalie?"

Luke squinted. "Who?"

The brothers exchanged curious looks.

Martin patted him again on the arm. "Don't worry, you will. Get some rest. We'll be back bright and early in the morning, okay?"

"Okay." Luke settled against the bed, closing his eyes.

"Night, Little Brother. We love you."

"Love you too."

Natalie checked the clock and scribbled more notes on the file before her. She extended it towards Melissa. The nurse continued to stare at her, hands still folded on the desk.

"I'm finished with this one."

"So, I see." Melissa took the file and placed it in the Inbox on the counter. "You would not believe some rumors that fly around this place."

"Wouldn't I?" Natalie muttered. She opened another file, scanning the contents. "I'm sure you'll let me know a juicy one."

"It's about you."

For the first time since she could remember, the curiosity bug bit her, and she allowed herself to act on it. Natalie leaned against the counter, cocking an eyebrow. "Okay, you got my attention. What about me?"

Melissa grinned. "Everyone's all abuzz about you and that Ward fellow."

"There is no me and that Ward fellow." Natalie shook her head. "I told you, he's not my boyfriend."

"Not that one! The younger one, Luke!"

She squinted. "What does that mean? In case you haven't noticed, he's been in a heavily medicated sleep for three days. It's not like we've gone on windy walks or to the movies."

Melissa surprised her by laughing. "I mean, look at the situation. Luke Ward comes in with no chance to live and survives surgery, only to suffer mild seizures and be placed in a medicated coma. What's the only thing that saves him?"

"The hospital and its-"

"You." Melissa poked in Natalie's direction with her pen. "You did, Natalie. You talked to him and touched him, so goes the rumor. I'm here to tell you. They didn't teach me those moves in nursing school." She propped her chin on her hand and fluttered her eyelashes. "You simply must share your secret."

"Don't be ridiculous." Natalie pushed away from the counter and gathered her folders with a flurry of hands. "That's the most asinine thing I've heard."

"I don't think I've ever heard you say that word before today."

She rolled her eyes. "There's a first time for everything."

Melissa shrugged, snatching up the phone as it rang. "Hold, please." She covered the phone with her hand. "You can protest all you want, but I vote the rumors are true. Visit Lover Boy while you've got the chance. I bet he's anxiously waiting on your return."

"Asinine." Natalie leaned over her desk. "You. Asinine." She pivoted and ran smack into Dr. Stewart. "Oh, Dr. S... Thomas, sorry I didn't see you there."

"It's perfectly alright." He glanced over at Melissa, busy on the phone. "Were you having a spelling bee?"

She scrunched up her nose. "No, it was nothing. Can I do something for you?"

"Yes, I'm headed to a meeting. Would you check up on Luke Ward for me? It might be time to clean him up and give him something other than liquid food."

Melissa coughed at the desk, covering her face with a folder.

Natalie fought the urge to roll her eyes again and nodded. "Sure thing, Doctor. It would be my pleasure."

"I bet."

They looked at Melissa, but she kept her gaze down, the phone pressed to her ear.

"I bet that was traumatic. Keep it well-cleaned and change the bandage once every three hours." She replaced the phone on the receiver and looked up at them with wide, innocent eyes. "What?"

"You can do this. It's just another patient." Natalie mumbled as she glared at the door number. "You are strong, intelligent, and ... talking to yourself."

She glanced over her shoulder to see several pairs of eyes locked on her. She turned away and straightened her shoulders. "You can do this. What's the big deal?" She entered the room to find the overhead lamp was on again. She let her eyes adjust before she stepped further into the room. She tried to be quiet as she noticed Luke still sleeping, moving to stand beside the bed.

She checked his vitals and reached down, picking up his wrist to time his pulse. It was strong and steady. She began to lower his hand back by his side. "Still looking good, Luke." She gasped when her wrist was suddenly captured by Luke's free hand. His firm grip surprised her, and her eyes flew to find his narrowed in on her, lips pressed firmly together.

"Who are you?"

"Mr. Ward, please let go of my wrist."

"Not until you answer me first." He squeezed her wrist. "Who are you?"

Natalie pulled to no avail. "I'm a nurse here." She relaxed and leaned her weight onto the bed without touching him further. "My name is Natalie. See?" She pointed to her name tag. "I work here as an RN. I've been looking after you since you got here. I let your brothers come in to see you and-"

Suddenly, he released her, and she stepped away, rubbing the skin of her wrist. "For a man in recovery, you have a strong grip."

"I-" He moaned, leaning back against the pillow.

His jaw clenched, and it was at that moment she noticed a thin sweat of perspiration on his brow. "Are you feeling okay?" She moved forward, reaching out to place a hand on his forehead, and studied his vitals. "Breathe and try to relax your muscles; you're having a muscle contraction." Her other hand checked his chest. "Does this hurt?" She pressed against his stomach, and he shook his head. She shifted her hand and pressed two fingers gently against his side. "This?"

He shook his head, eyes watching her. "No."

"Are you breathing for me?"

"Of course, I'm breathing. I-" He flinched again, and her eyes narrowed. She moved her hand and let it hover above the right side of his pelvis. "What the hell are you- Hey!"

"There?"

"Yes! Ow, stop!"

She removed her touch from him completely, and he shifted uncomfortably on the bed as he glared at her.

"You need to urinate, Mr. Ward," she looked away, "and whatever else you feel necessary. I'll call in a couple of male nurses to help you."

He was ignoring her at this point, a faint blush coating his cheeks. She chose to say nothing else, simply exiting the room without another word.

Thirty minutes later, Natalie found Luke propped up against his pillows, a frown on his handsome face. She cleared her throat, shoving a lock of hair behind her ear. "Is everything okay, Mr. Ward?"

"My name is Luke."

"Luke, do you need anything?"

"I don't need another male helping me piss and shit. Who the Hell invented the fucking bedpan?"

"I'm afraid I don't know the answer to that. I can get you something to eat or..."

"I'm not hungry."

"Surely, you must-"

"I said I'm not hungry."

Natalie crossed her arms. "Listen to me, Luke, and listen carefully. You will eat it whether you like it or not, and yes, it will be nasty cafeteria food. Your brothers have been here day and night since you arrived, worrying themselves sick over you. I will get you better if it's the last thing I do!"

He was staring at her with that look from before, and she paused at the intensity of it, shifting nervously on her feet.

"What are you-"

"I've heard your voice."

"I told you who I was. I sat with you..."

"I thought I was crazy, but you were real all along." He shook his head. "You told me to come back."

"You found your way through the darkness, Luke." She disagreed with a shake of her head. "I happened to be at the end of that tunnel, along with your family."

He scoffed. "You told me to come back to you, and I did... only to find no you."

"You're obviously a bit drowsy from the meds you were given earlier, and you're regaining a sense of balance. How about I bring you back something warm from the cafeteria?"

He said nothing, merely crossing his arms, and winced. She was halfway out the door when his voice stopped her. "You wouldn't be able to sneak me a smoke, would you?"

She threw him a look over her shoulder. "Maybe you'd like me to get one of the male nurses and check your colon?"

He rolled his eyes. "Fine."

She heard him grumbling as she made her way towards the elevator.

"Didn't want a cigarette anyway."

CHAPTER SIX

"I hear the Ward boy is up and kicking."

Natalie grabbed a small travel-size container of milk from the cafeteria freezer. "He's got a cranky attitude, but that's to be expected. The medication is wearing off, and he's no longer asleep to not notice it."

Seventh-floor Doctor Larissa Shevitz nodded and grabbed a small container of orange juice. "Dr. Stewart informs me you're the only RN on the sixth floor. That's quite an accomplishment, considering you're the only nurse the Ward kid has."

Natalie frowned. "I wasn't aware of that."

"I thought you were informed. The eighth floor had a bit of a fire problem today, and to everyone's panic, an escape from their psych center. Dr. Stewart had to relocate several nurses on each floor to help." Dr. Shevitz gazed at Natalie with sympathetic eyes. "Your floor only has Diane, Melissa, and Reba now. I have a minimum of seven patients every two hours. Four of those are already in-house patients."

"I heard." Dr. Shevitz shook her head. "Hence me thinking you already knew!"

Natalie cleared her throat and shot the doctor a smile. "If you'll excuse me, Dr. Shevitz, I must return to my floor."

"Of course, Dear."

She paid quickly, making her way towards the elevators, and was back on her floor before she had time to recollect herself. She brushed her face with the sleeve of her scrubs, stepped off the elevator, and instantly collided with the person standing there.

"I'm sorry I..."

"Was too busy crying to notice me standing here."

Her head shot up, eyes landing on Martin. "Oh, hello."

He eyed her closely, eyebrows furrowed. "Why are you crying?"

She motioned him out of the elevator, smiling at a passing nurse, and brushed her face one final time. "No reason."

"Don't lie." Martin stretched his arm out to place his hand on the wall. He wasn't trapping her in completely, but his muscular frame made it impossible for her to step around him without touching him. "I don't like seeing ladies cry. Tell me what's wrong."

"I've had a hard day, okay? They keep throwing all this shit at me because I never say no." She grumbled as she clutched the food tray in her hands. "This hospital is my job, and I love it, but it's become my life." She met his gaze. "My day off with you was the first time I had a nice lunch with someone not working here or just me."

"You're wearing yourself out, Sweetheart." Martin reached out to stroke her cheek. "What do you say you let me take you to dinner?"

"Nurse Hamilton?"

She jolted at his touch, eyes wide as she spotted Dr. Stewart. "Yes, Doctor?"

"Everything okay?"

She blushed and jerked stray hair behind her ears. "Yes, perfectly alright. I was about to deliver some food to Mr. Ward."

He eyed Martin but nodded. "I'll leave you to it." He checked his watch. "I want you to take off early. You've been here too long."

"Dr. Stewart, I can..."

"I mean it." He glanced towards Martin. "Make sure she heeds my command."

Martin grinned. "Yes, Sir."

Dr. Stewart disappeared into the hallway, and Natalie jerked her gaze over at Martin to find him still grinning at her.

"I'm glad you find it funny."

"I didn't say it was funny. It's more like perfect timing."

"Dinner doesn't happen at eight in the morning, Martin."

"No, but breakfast does."

She shook her head, unable to fight the smile that appeared as she approached Luke's room, Martin following close behind. "Your brother is beyond cranky." She paused with her hand on the doorknob. "Is he usually that way?"

"Cranky?" He shook his head. "Nah, he's usually drunk or acting spaced out."

Natalie chuckled, and they entered the room to find Luke sitting up, his arms crossed. He glanced between the two of them. "You guys go to Egypt to get my food?"

"Do you even know where Egypt is Lukey-Poo?"

"Up your ass," Luke pointed down with his middle finger, "And around the corner," He twisted it, bringing his finger up birdie style. "See?"

Natalie glanced at Martin with a funny look. "See what I mean? Cranky!"

"Hey! You try being stuck in this bed while strangers wipe your ass for you and be forced to eat shitty food for fifty days straight and see how you like it. I bet you'd be cranky, too."

"You've been here for four days, Luke." Natalie moved forward, propped the legs on the tray, and set it over his lap.

"That's right, Little Brother. Four. Not fifty, way to count."

The younger Ward glanced down at his plate, eyes narrowing at the sight of the triangular-cut turkey sandwich, the apple set to the side, and the milk container. "Was this all they had?"

Martin glared. "It was all you could afford at the free table."

"If you don't want it..."

Luke must have heard the hurt in her voice. His gaze snapped up to connect with hers. He quickly shook his head, scooting the tray closer. "No, this is great. Thank you."

"If you need anything else, don't hesitate to hit your call button. We're a little stretched thin on staff, but I'll try to get here as quickly as possible."

"Yeah, uh, thanks again."

Satisfied, she moved past Martin back into the hallway, pausing outside the door when he caught up with her, grabbing her elbow.

"I meant what I said about taking you out for breakfast. I'll be waiting when you get off."

Natalie opened her mouth to protest but quickly shut it before nodding.

"Great. See you in the morning."

Her eyes went past him to see Luke watching the two of them curiously. When he saw he had been caught, he whipped his gaze back down at his plate.

"Okay, Martin." Natalie moved into the hallway. "See you at eight."

Natalie buttoned her jacket against her chest, shoving her hands into the pockets, and she turned towards the hospital entrance after hearing the doors slide open. Martin made his way up to her, fixing leather gloves onto his hands, and he added the black beanie on his head. He smiled as he stopped beside her. "Ready?"

"Sure, where are you taking me?"

"You like breakfast, right? I thought we'd hit up a local pancake house."

She hesitated as her stomach rumbled loudly. She blushed. "It sounds perfect."

The drive to the restaurant was only fifteen minutes away. Natalie glanced around as they sat at a nonsmoking table near the back. She smiled as she took the menu handed to her, and the petite blonde informed them she'd return soon to take their orders. The waitress left, drawing her attention to the menu's pictures and information. She knew Martin hadn't opened his menu and instead settled back in the chair, watching her.

She lowered her menu. "Something on your mind?"

"I can't help but think how lucky I am in many ways. Ma used to tell me everything happens for a reason, but the day Luke almost died, I didn't believe that anymore." He cleared his throat. "You showed up, and Luke started fighting back."

"Martin-"

"Let me finish. Now he's awake and talking to us. In a way, he's the same old Luke, but I can see a different part of him." Martin fiddled with his fork. "I can see it when he looks at you."

"I don't know what you mean."

"You don't see it, but I do. You should have heard him talking when he first woke up. He thought you were a voice commanding him to come back. I think a small part of him believed you wanted him to return for you. I'm puzzled as to why he would think that."

She shifted in her seat but kept her eyes on him. "I was in the room with him when he woke up, like Dr. Stewart told you. I was talking to him, and he happened to be on a level of subconscious where he could hear me."

"Say I believe that. Why would he fight so hard because of that? What'd you say to him?"

"It was a normal conversation. I held his hand like I usually do with patients." Natalie shrugged. "I remember telling him he needed to come back, that you were all worried about him, and that it was time to come back to me. I didn't say..." She paused and bit her bottom lip.

"I think Luke took that a little more personally than it really is."

"Of course, he must have. I don't even really know him."

"Can I ask you something personal?"

She sat back in the booth. "Sure, I guess. Go ahead."

"Are you attracted to my brother at all?"

With wide eyes, she stared at him. "What kind of question is that? Your brother has been in the hospital vulnerable for days, and you're trying to hook him up?"

"No." Martin leaned forward. "I'm asking because I didn't want to get in the way if you liked him, even in the slightest bit. Luke has a way of tricking women by looking cute and helpless all the time. He hasn't mastered the whole manly thing."

"Are you saying you want to date me?"

He chuckled. "Since you cut to the chase, that's what I'm saying."

The waitress returned, and Natalie focused her attention on her menu with shaky hands. They ordered, sitting in silence until the food arrived. When they began to eat, Martin glanced every so often at her. She concentrated entirely on her food. She didn't focus back on him until they were finished.

Natalie wiped her mouth with her napkin. She cleared her throat. "I don't think that's such a good idea, Martin."

Eyebrows furrowed, he stared at her. "And why not?"

"The hospital has strict policies against..."

"This has nothing to do with the hospital, Natalie. For once, separate yourself from what the hospital demands of you. This is about me wanting to date you, the woman, not the nurse."

She toyed with her napkin. "I don't think I'm ready for a relationship. I'm at the hospital constantly; they depend on me, and even though it sometimes stresses me out, it's my life. It's all I've ever had that made me feel like I was important and useful. That's the only side of me you've ever seen because there is no other me. That's all there is."

"Give me a chance, and I'll show you that you're wrong."

Natalie cursed under her breath as she felt her bottom lip tremble. "I don't know if I can. I'm scared."

"I know." He dug for his wallet, threw a large bill on the table, and stood up. "Come on, let's go."

Without a sound, she buttoned her coat, thanked the waitress, and followed him to his car. The ride back to the hospital was silent, and he remained quiet as he pulled into the parking garage beside her car.

"Thanks for breakfast, Martin." Natalie didn't meet his eyes and climbed from the car's passenger side, shutting the door as quickly as she retrieved her keys. She paused, hearing Martin's door open and shut. She fully faced the direction of his car in time to see him come from around the back bumper towards her. "Is everything al-"

Martin gently cupped her face with both hands, carefully giving her space to step back. "We're all scared to some extent, Natalie. I was afraid you'd automatically say no, but you didn't. You fought with saying yes, and that gave me hope that somewhere inside, you wanted to agree."

"Martin-"

"And that's a good enough answer for me." He captured her mouth in a firm kiss, and she stiffened against him. Her eyes fluttered shut. Her hand dropped her keys unnoticed at her feet as she allowed herself to grip the front of his jacket.

Martin broke the kiss. He smiled at the dazed expression on her face. She maintained a firm group on his jacket, eyelids opening, and he could see the swirl of emotions in her green eyes. A car alarm went off somewhere in the depths of the garage, and Natalie stepped away from him.

"I'm sorry, I ... I shouldn't of..." She rubbed her forehead. "You kissed me."

"You kissed me back." He shoved his hands into the pockets of his jacket. "I'd like to kiss you again."

Her gaze went to his again. The seconds ticked by like molasses. He was surprised when she slowly nodded, the daze obvious in her eyes.

Two Months Later

"Stop." Natalie wagged her finger. "I'm on the clock," she hissed, looking around. "People will see you."

"See me do what? This?" Martin pulled her close to hug her and grinned as she giggled, trying harmlessly to shove him away.

"I mean it, Martin." She laughed. "Let go!"

"When you guys are done... with whatever that's called, I'd like to get out of here."

She pushed him away, ignoring his wide grin, and blushed. She shoved her hair behind her ears. "I'm sorry, Luke. You must be past ready."

He stood in the doorway of his room and adjusted the grip on the bag in his hand. "Yeah, I'm more than ready to get home." He looked surprised when she threw her arms around his neck. He shot Martin a confused look, who only grinned in return, and he allowed his free arm to hug her back without much pressure.

"I'm going to miss seeing you every day." She squeezed his neck and stepped back. "It won't be the same without hearing you complain about taking your medication or the snide remarks about how much you hate the food."

"Nonsense," Martin snorted. "You'll be at the house as much as him, Nat. You'll have a lot of time to hear him complain about Destiny's cooking."

She blushed as she remembered it had been two nights since she had gone home, her bag of belongings still in his room. Since the day he kissed her, he hardly left her alone, asking her on many dates and showing up at all hours at the hospital. Eventually, she started hanging out with him and his family at their house. It progressed to staying a night or two from time to time. They hadn't slept together, not that he hadn't tried, but he had been respectful of her.

She cleared her throat. "It won't be every day."

Martin chuckled, giving her a knowing look before he motioned at Luke. "Come on, Little Brother. Time to get you home." He leaned over to kiss her cheek, ignoring her protests, as Melissa shouted something behind the station counter. "I'll pick you up when you get off in the morning."

"Okay. Luke, don't forget to schedule your first therapy session appointment."

With a short nod, he didn't look at her. "Fine."

"Take your meds on time, every day, as directed." Natalie bit her lower lip. "And don't hesitate to call me if you need anything, like... you know, hospital-wise." She shrugged. "Or if you need to talk."

His head lifted, watchful eyes catching her own, and he slung his bag strap onto his left shoulder. "I will, Natalie."

She moved forward to hug him again, and this time, he wrapped both arms around her before pulling away. "Now, go home and drive at a safe speed." She poked Martin in the stomach. "I don't want to see this boy in our OR again."

"You got it." He dug out his car keys. "Let's go, Luke."

She watched in silence while they walked past her. They entered the elevator, Martin leaning to press the garage floor button. He raised his hand as the doors shut. Luke remained beside him with his gaze directed on the floor. She turned back to the desk. She ignored Melissa's wide grin and opened the file with her name. "Stop staring at me like that."

Melissa leaned back in her chair and motioned with wiggling fingers at Nurse Cook. "You owe me money."

Natalie raised her eyebrows. "Why?"

"Because it only took the Ward boy two months to woo you instead of three."

"You took bets?"

"How could I not?" Melissa laughed. "It was impossible not to, especially with all your speeches every time I saw you. Admit it, that man had your number day one."

"Whatever." Natalie rolled her eyes but couldn't help the smile that appeared. She focused back on the folder's contents.

Melissa chuckled and accepted the twenty dollars from Nurse Cook. "So, is he a considerate lover or a real beast between the sheets?" She wiggled her eyebrows as she waved the money before her nose. "Wait, let me guess. He's both."

She felt her face flame red, refusing to look back at Melissa, and bit her lower lip. "I wouldn't know."

"Two months, and you don't know?"

She looked up to see them staring at her. "I haven't slept with him."

"Damn it." Melissa rolled her eyes and handed the money back to Nurse Cook.

CHAPTER SEVEN

Martin turned up the car heater and shot her a look. The vehicle rolled down the road. He threw his right arm over the back of her seat. "What's wrong, Nat?"

She shifted in the seat to make sure the seat belt was secure. "It was a long shift, that's all."

"Did you get more patients or something?"

"No, it was more like certain people were riding my ass all day kind of something," she grumbled.

"Who?" His eyes narrowed. He glanced between her and the road. "Was it people that work with you? They got names?"

She couldn't help but giggle. "Of course, they have names." She crossed her arms and leaned back in her seat. "It's Melissa and some other ladies, that's all. They've been asking me things about you." She swung her head towards him. "Damn it, Martin. I told you not to do that stuff at work!"

"Whoa, Babe." He chuckled and threw up his free hand as if in surrender. "Not that I don't think you're smoking hot when you're angry, but hold up a minute. I didn't see a problem with giving you a hug in front of them. They're family to you. It's not like they cared."

"They're taking bets on how long until we sleep together and...."

"Wait, what'd you tell them?"

"What did I tell them? I told them the truth!"

"You tell them how long my-"

"Martin!"

With a grin, he moved his hand to grip the back of her neck, massaging her with his fingers in slow circles. "I'm teasing you. So, what if they're curious? They tease you like I do my brothers."

She relaxed against the warmth of his hand. "I don't see where it's any of their business. I doubt they'll ask now that I told them you have an erection problem."

He slammed the brakes right in front of the house. "My what?"

Natalie gazed at him with wide eyes. "It's okay; they understand since they're nurses. It happens a lot, especially with men your age."

"Natalie, I'm about to turn this car around. I'll prove I don't have an... an erection problem to all of 'em. I swear it!"

She couldn't hold it in any longer, peals of laughter escaping her. She fanned her face and laughed every time she saw his expression.

He watched her for several minutes before realization dawned on him. "Very funny, Tinkerbell."

"I was only teasing you, Martin. Turnabout is fair play, and don't call me that."

"Why?" He grinned and cut off the engine. "You look like the cute little pixie from Peter Pan."

They climbed out of the car, and he came to her side, throwing his arm around her neck to pull her close and press his lips against her temple.

"Watch yourself," Natalie grumbled with a smile.

He chuckled, kissing her temple again, and they climbed the steps, a shower of voices greeting them. Martin shut the door and shrugged off his jacket. He took hers to hang up, and she smiled at Destiny, the woman fussing at Martin for tracking snow in the house. He began to fight with her playfully. Natalie shook her head and stepped towards the living room. Her eyes fell on the back of Luke's head as she approached from behind him, the television playing a music video.

She moved around the couch to take a seat beside him. "I like Smells like Teen Spirit, but that wasn't their best song."

He kept his eyes on the screen. "I didn't peg you as a Nirvana fan."

"I had a roommate who loved them back in college. Are you a huge fan?" He changed the channel. He stopped on another music video by some band she didn't recognize. She shifted beside him, clearing her throat as silence crawled between them. Her fingers tapped on the sides of her thighs. "Did you eat already? Need any medication or-"

"I'm fine."

"Well, if you want, I can-"

"We're not at the hospital anymore. You're not on the clock. There's no need to hover over me, okay?"

"Luke, I-"

"Forget it, okay? Just leave me alone for a bit." He shoved off the couch, moving too fast, and hissed between his teeth. He paused, right hand moving to clutch at his shoulder.

Natalie sprung to her feet and wrapped an arm around his waist. She steadied him with her free hand on his chest, spreading her feet for balance, and most of his weight leaned against her. "It's okay. Breathe, Sweetheart."

The muscle in his cheek jumped as he clenched his jaw, but he nodded, his hand resting over hers on his chest.

"Little Brother, you okay?" Martin was suddenly at their side, a concerned look on his face, Warrick and Destiny close behind him.

Stepping away from Natalie, he nodded. "Yeah, I got up too fast, that's all."

"Good thing my girl is here to look after your slow ass." Martin teased, ruffling Luke's hair with a grin. He threw an arm around Natalie to bring her closer. "We might have to start paying you extra for taking care of Luke here."

"No extra pay needed," she whispered. Luke's gaze found hers again. "I'm concerned because I care, not because it's my job."

"You're one of a kind." Martin pressed a kiss against her temple before he stepped away, clapping his hands together. "I say we all sit down together tonight and have a family dinner. What'd you guys think?"

"That sounds good to me," Warrick nodded. "I'm hungry."

"Man, you're always hungry."

"Growing men got to eat."

"Yeah, but you're growing out, not up."

"You be quiet about my man, Martin." Destiny pointed at him. "You don't have to be rude to him all the time just because he's better-looking than you."

"You're jealous your boyfriend's prettier than you."

"If you two are done complimenting each other," Natalie interrupted with a smile, "Luke might want some help to his room."

"I'm going to go get a spiral ham." Martin rubbed his stomach. "Rick, you and your bodyguard help Luke up the stairs."

"I'm not letting you pick the ham by yourself," Warrick shook his head. "The last one you picked looked like it had fought a boxing match with Mike Tyson. I'm coming with you," he shot a look at Destiny when she glared at him and crossed her arms, "and so is Destiny."

"Then who will..."

"I'll help him." Natalie cleared her throat. "You guys do whatever it is that makes you feel macho. I'm sure Destiny will make sure we get a good ham."

"You bet. Come on, Boys."

Seconds later, his car pulled away from the curb, and she shut the door. She came back into the living room and found it empty. "Luke?" Frowning, she stepped back towards the foyer. "Where'd you go?" She ducked into the hallway, eyes widening at seeing him on the stairs. "Luke, what in the world are you doing?" She rushed up the three steps to his side. "I said I'd help you."

"I don't need the help."

She could see he was already sweating from exertion, hands on the rails to either side of him. "The way your body is reacting, I'd say you do."

"My body? What-" He tossed a glare at her from over his shoulder. "My body is fine. Don't touch me, okay?"

"I said I'd help you, and that's what I'm going to do." She squeezed under his left arm, coming up to rest under it, and threw an arm around his waist. "Lean on me for support, and keep your weight on your left leg." She gripped the back of his shirt with her fingers. "It'll be a piece of cake, I promise." She looked up with a smile and froze at the sight of him looking down at her.

His head was tilted down, dark eyes locked on her face, but she knew without hesitation that he wasn't looking into her eyes. At first, she wasn't even sure it was her he was seeing, the expression in his eyes indescribable. She felt the warm breath of his mouth hit her cheek and blinked out of her stupor. "Luke? Are you ready to start?"

He curled his arm around her hand, cupping the top of her shoulder, and he nodded. They began up the steps at a slow, careful pace.

"Natalie?"

"Yes, Luke?" She kept her eyes on the stairs and watched their feet.

"Would you lie to Martin and tell him I did this on my own?"

"What happens if I do, and he won't help you up the next time?"

"I'm sure I can make up something to make him feel manly for helping me." He sighed in relief when his feet landed flat on the top step. He smiled. "It really is good to be home."

She slipped out from under his arm. "I'm glad to see you back here too." She lingered behind him as he limped into his room, mindful of the cast on his leg. He sat on his bed, but she remained in the hallway. "I don't mean to hover or suffocate you. I worry about you, that's all."

"I get it was your job, Natalie, but we're not at the hospital anymore. You don't need to feel obligated." He slid back to the wall, and she moved into his room. He silently watched her sit down cross-legged. She lifted his left foot into her lap and began to untie his shoelaces.

She was aware he continued to watch her, and she undid the laces with her head down. She removed the shoe and placed it beside his bed before shifting his foot back to the carpet. She lifted her eyes to his. "Is there anything I can do for you while I'm up here?"

"You can get out."

Eyes wide, Natalie jerked back. "Excuse me?"

Luke nudged his head towards his door. "You heard me."

She shifted back on her knees, moving her hands to rest on her thighs. "Luke, I know that you're hurting, but-"

"I said, get out." He pointed at the door. "Get out of my room!"

Scrambling to her feet, she was halfway down the stairs when she heard him slam the door shut. She flew down the last steps and covered her mouth with a shaking hand. She threw her other arm out to support herself against the wall. She went into the bathroom without knowing why so he wouldn't hear her cry.

She didn't come out until she heard the group return an hour later. She could hear loud music coming from Luke's room, and she wiped her face with the towel before she stepped out to greet them.

Martin eyed her but thankfully said nothing. A gasp escaped her when she spotted the massive ham amongst several grocery bags.

"What'd you guys do? Buy out the whole store?"

Warrick glanced at her and frowned. He exchanged a look with Martin. Without a word, he turned to help Destiny get items out of the bags.

Martin slapped the ham proudly. "Best-looking ham in the whole damn place. I picked it myself."

Destiny snorted but didn't turn away from the sink.

"I'm sure you did." Natalie smiled. She glanced around. "What can I do to help?"

"You can sit back and enjoy yourself." He pulled her close and glanced over to see Destiny and Warrick were busy. "Is everything okay?" He whispered in her ear. "You've been crying."

"What?" She pulled back, "No, I haven't. I'm fine."

He cocked an eyebrow. He took her hand and pulled her into the foyer. "Don't lie to me, Sweetheart." He cornered her, successfully trapping her against a wall with both arms. "I know you well enough by now to know when you're not honest with me. What happened? Did you fight with Luke? You know better than all of us how cranky he gets on that medication."

"I'm fine," she whispered. "We didn't fight. He's tired, that's all. Poor thing made it almost all the way up the stairs by himself. I wasn't helping by hovering over him."

"You're only trying to help him. He should appreciate you a bit more." Martin sighed and pushed away to rub at the bridge of his nose. "You've done a lot for that boy, and he's not been nice to you. It would be best if you guys had some one-on-one time, so you two can get to know each other better. He'll be less cranky if that happened."

"I don't know if that's such a good idea, Martin. I mean-"

"Don't be silly, Nat. You're a part of this family now, and since I'm hoping you might be around more often, I think getting to know you would be the best thing for Luke. Have you ever told him you know how to play the guitar?"

She shook her head. "Be around more?" She frowned, but it was replaced with a hesitant smile. "Why would you say that?"

His grin widened, and he moved his hands to the wall behind her. "Because I like having you next to me when I wake up in the mornings."

She glanced over his shoulder towards the kitchen. "Don't talk so loud."

"Why?" He chuckled. "Cause of Warrick and Destiny? Please. I've already told them if they hear a loud thump, that it's us."

"You did not!"

He nodded. "I just don't tell them that it's usually you kicking me off the bed in your sleep."

"I like my apartment. It's the first thing I started paying for on my own."

"Keep it if you want, Baby." He brushed his lips against hers. "Say yes." Her eyes closed as she felt his teeth pull at her lower lip. "Say yes, Natalie."

She let out something between a sigh and a moan at the feeling of his fingers skimming down the side of her torso. His hand shifted down to grip her waist. He stepped forward, bringing them closer, as he bent his arm that still rested against the wall. Natalie opened her eyes at the feeling of his fingers slipping under her shirt.

"Martin?"

He looked up from over his arm, eyebrows raised, and Natalie immediately stepped away to brush her shaking hands over her shirt.

"Yeah, what is it?"

Luke glared down at them from the top of the stairs. "Would you mind bringing me some water?" His eyes stayed locked on Martin. "I need to take a pill."

"Sure thing, Little Brother. Be right there." Martin stepped back and shot her an apologetic look. "Hold that thought, Nat." He disappeared into the kitchen.

Luke stared at her, squeezing the wood of the railing for a split second before he turned and disappeared back into his room. The door slammed loudly behind him.

Frowning, she ventured back into the kitchen.

The house was quiet when she opened her eyes and rolled over to look at the clock on the nightstand. The blaring red numbers proclaimed it was barely three in the morning. She rubbed at the sleep that had collected around the corner of her eyelids and glanced over her shoulder to see Martin sleeping beside her, clad only in his boxer shorts. She smiled, remembering how he had argued for days about being allowed to wear whatever he wanted to bed. She forced him to vow to everyone that he had no dishonorable intentions of being almost naked next to her and that it wasn't a smooth sex move. Just watching him raise his hand and state it aloud to Warrick and Tony had been enough for her to agree after she stopped dying laughing.

She was too scared to tell him the real reason was that she had only been with one man sexually, not because she wanted to wait until the time was right. She had been on dates and done other things with men; she wasn't naïve despite only being twenty-three, but Martin was a different type of man altogether. He knew what he was doing, had been with women who knew exactly how to give him what he wanted, and the idea of disappointing him scared her.

Some of her hesitated because she wasn't sure if sleeping with him would be the right decision. Fear gripped her each time she thought about it. What if he got what he wanted and then no longer wanted her? The thought almost made her hate herself. Of course, Martin wasn't like that. It didn't stop her from thinking about it.

A part of her believed being in any relationship was an unwise decision. Nothing lasted forever. Why should she believe that this would? What if Martin found someone else? Did she love him? Was it too early to think that? She wasn't sure she knew what love was or what it felt like other than what she had seen in movies or read in books.

Natalie slid from the bed, careful not to wake him, as she closed the door to his room. She ignored the goose bumps that crawled down at her arms, scolding herself for not grabbing a robe. She descended the stairs in a black tank top and matching shorts. Not that they were indecent, but it bothered her that she didn't have anything to cover up with in case someone had the same idea. Quietly, she grabbed a cup from the cabinet and filled it with milk. Her nanny used to give her a glass of milk when she couldn't sleep.

The warm memories brought a smile to her face, and Natalie sipped at the milk in the darkened kitchen, only beams of moonlight allowing her to see what she was doing. Finishing, she rinsed the cup and placed it in the sink. She was slow and careful, making her way back up the stairs.

Hand on the doorknob of Martin's room, she paused at hearing a muffled sound from Luke's room. Instantly concerned, she inched forward. She pressed her ear against his door, hands flat against the door frame. It was unmistakable, his low groan of pain, and as carefully as she could, she cracked open the door to stick her head inside.

The room was dark except for the moonlight from the window. She could see Luke on the bed, the outline of his face visible, with half of it shadowed and tilted away from the window. He was sweating, and she watched him shudder, mumbling incoherently to himself. Another groan escaped him, and she ducked back out into the hallway.

She returned with a damp rag from the bathroom and shut his door behind her, inching towards his bed. "Luke?" He didn't answer, and she lowered herself to her knees. Steadying her hand, she leaned over to brush the hair from his forehead. She frowned at the heat that came off his skin. He was burning up with a fever.

Natalie brushed the rag against his face, and the cool sensation caused him to sigh, tilting his head towards her in his sleep. She wiped his forehead once again. His body began to stop shaking. She placed the rag on the floor and rearranged his blankets to cover him. His chest rose and fell in a steady pattern. She tucked the sheets in around his torso, mindful of the bandages and his cast.

Luke remained asleep. She was content for a few minutes to sit back and watch him. He looked just like the first time she saw him: young, helpless... Cute. She scolded herself. No, she couldn't think that way.

He mumbled again, and she froze at the sound of her name. Eyes wide, she leaned back to see his fingers twitching, and unable to help herself, she inched her fingers towards his hand. She held her breath and slipped her hand into his, watching the long fingers curl and tighten around her own. Her eyes lingered on their joined hands.

"Natalie." Her gaze rose, the robust features of his face magnified by the moonlight. "Natalie, you're not there." His fingers twitched, his breath catching, as a muscle spasmodically jerked in his chest. "Not mine."

She covered her mouth with her free hand. Trying to control her emotions, she looked away and rubbed the tears that had gathered around her eyes. She began to remove her hand from his. Natalie paused at the feeling of his grip tightening. After a brief, torturous second, he relaxed but didn't let go. She raised her free hand again to brush her fingertips across his forehead. "Luke, let go. You have to let me go." He mumbled something she couldn't make out clearly. "Luke, let go." She was close to him now, almost leaning against the pillow supporting his head. "It's time to let me go now."

His grip went lax, and she looked down at her free hand, rubbing at her wrist. Smiling, she looked towards the sleeping man. She froze when their eyes met.

"What are you doing in my room?"

"You were in pain," she stuttered. "I thought you might need my help."

Luke grunted and slid back to lean against his pillow.

He reached to snap on the lamp, and she blinked rapidly against the sudden brightness. She was suddenly all too aware of her state of dress, and she cleared her throat nervously, not daring to move as he continued to stare at her. "Do you need anything? I brought you a wet washcloth. You have a bit of a fever."

He took it from her without a word, hand squeezing it tightly. He didn't as water seeped from the material and ran down his fingers onto the bed.

"Do you want some water? I could get you some Tylenol. I have some that might help you sleep."

"I want you to get out."

"Not until I help you," the firmness in her voice surprised her, "and don't tell me you don't need it because that's bullshit. You do."

His right eyebrow rose at her, but he said nothing.

"You need to take something if you're in pain, and I'm here now. I'll get it for you."

"I'm not in pain." He tossed the washcloth onto the dirty clothes-basket at the foot of the bed. "I was having a nightmare."

"What kind of nightmare?"

He looked away. "Why do you care? Shouldn't you be with Martin right now?"

"Martin doesn't need me, Luke, you do." She was hesitant but reached out nonetheless, placing a hand gently on his arm. "I want to help you, but you have to trust me, and let me do that. Don't you see that I care about you?"

His gaze lifted to hers. "I don't need anything from you." H watched a look of hurt flash across her face again, "I don't want medicine." He cleared his throat. "I'd like my phone and earbuds on the shelf behind me."

"Of course, Luke." She moved forward to take a seat on the edge of his bed. He made room, shifting towards the wall, and she tried to ignore his gaze. She reached over his left shoulder and spotted the phone next to Bluetooth earbuds. She felt his weight shift, and concerned, she looked down. "Are you sure you're-" Her eyes locked on his as he studied her, their faces inches apart.

He had inched upwards to sit taller against the pillow, and it caused her to press her chest against him from the angle. She slipped from surprise. Flustered, she reached out to grab the top of the shelf, and the movement only brought her closer to him. She felt his hand slip between them to rest on the naked curve of her hip and inhaled sharply. "Luke..."

Before she could untangle herself, he captured her mouth with his. Shock made her fall even more against him. His tongue brushed against her own, his hand slipping under her tank top, and he pressed her against him. She returned the kiss, and he deepened it. Her hand slipped from the shelf to slide up his shoulder, her fingers digging into the choppy hair at the base of his neck.

Everything in her brain was screaming at that very moment, warning bells and alarms whistling, but they were drowned out by the sound of her heart beating rapidly against her chest. Someone moaned, she wasn't sure whom, and she gasped into his mouth as his hand slipped around the front to cover one of her breasts. He squeezed, thumb flicking against her hardening nipple, and she jerked against him. She heard him chuckle, smiling against her lips, and he changed direction of his hand, skimming down her stomach quickly. She gasped at feeling his hand slide down the front of her shorts.

Natalie tore her mouth from his, releasing his hair so fast she swayed back and grabbed at his shoulder to steady herself. Luke hissed in pain, and she fell from the bed. "I'm sorry. I didn't mean to. Are you okay? I'm so sorry."

Luke pushed her hand away and shook his head. "No, I'm fine. Just go."

"But-"

"Go." He turned his head away. "Please."

Heart thumping against her chest, she scrambled to her feet. The door shut behind her within seconds. Natalie leaned against the door, and it took several minutes to collect her composure.

Slow, careful steps took her back into Martin's room, and she slipped back under the covers. She turned away from him, curling herself into a little ball. Her eyes found the red lights of the clock, and she fixed her gaze on them, never again finding the sleep she so desperately needed.

CHAPTER EIGHT

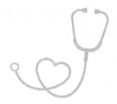

M artin reached out for Natalie. His search came up empty, the cool sheets drifting under his fingertips. He swung his legs off the bed, stretching, before he grabbed a pair of worn jeans from the floor. He found Warrick and Destiny in the living room. The television was on, not that it mattered. It was apparent they weren't paying any attention to it.

He scratched at his stomach with a yawn. "You guys seen Natalie?" He heard the back door of the house open and turned to see Natalie entering and brushing snow off her coat. "Hey, I woke up, and you were gone. You had me worried."

She flashed him an uneasy smile. She slid her jacket off her shoulders and entered the foyer to put it on the coat rack. "Sorry, it looked so nice outside. I wanted to go for a walk."

"Nice, my ass," Warrick yelled from the living room. "Girl, you probably froze your titties off." There was a loud slapping sound, and he grunted. "Geez, Woman, that hurt."

Martin shook his head in amusement. "Are you hungry? Do you want something to eat?"

"I'm not hungry right now, but closer to lunchtime, I might be."

He reached out to pull her close and frowned when she went stiff against him. "You are sure that you're okay?"

"Yeah, fine." She sent him another small smile and backed away. "You mentioned food. If you and Warrick are hungry, I'm sure I can make you something to eat."

He cocked an eyebrow and followed her into the kitchen. "Yeah, that sounds good. You forgot the rock star upstairs."

"Oh, right, Luke. I didn't mean to forget him." Natalie muttered with a nod. She concentrated on gathering things in the kitchen. "I'll get started."

Martin stretched again. "I'm gonna go jump in the shower. I'll see if he's up. Maybe this time I can get his ass downstairs in one non-cranky piece."

"Okay."

He slipped out of the kitchen, and the room went silent while she retrieved plates from the cabinet. Destiny appeared and retrieved the ingredients from the fridge. The sound of the hockey game floated into the kitchen, and she smiled at hearing him cuss when the other team scored. The sound of something hitting the television echoed into the room. Destiny moved to stand beside her, opening the bread bag, but Natalie was aware that the woman was concentrating on more than just the bag.

"You've done a lot for Luke."

Natalie shrugged, accepting the slice of bread handed. She gripped the knife and dipped it into the jar of mustard on the counter. "I was his nurse. Like I keep saying, it was my job."

"He thinks a lot of you, you know."

"Who, Martin?" Natalie wiggled her nose, placing the bread on the plate.

Destiny didn't extend the next piece of bread right away. "No, Luke thinks a lot of you." She thrust the slice of bread out. "This conversation is about you and Luke."

Natalie slathered the next piece with a glob of mustard. "There is no me and Luke."

"I see the way he looks at you. Last night, it was plain as day. You should have seen his face, the way he looked at you when you helped him from the couch. No, wait," she tapped at her chin, "you did see that."

Natalie placed down the knife and turned to gaze at her. She exhaled at the look the woman was giving her, not one of hostility but one of sympathy. "Destiny, please don't tell Martin. Luke's -"

"He's in love with you."

She leaned against the counter, rubbing her forehead. "I don't know how this happened. I haven't done anything to my knowledge that would make him feel that way, have I?"

"Feel what way?" Her eyes swung to the doorway to see Warrick leaning against it with a frown. He glanced between them. "What are you talking about?"

"The king of the crank, Rick!" Destiny threw her hands up, glancing at Natalie, and returned to the counter. "It's like you men have no ears. Natalie's upset because Luke has been rude to her lately."

"He's reacting to the medication," Natalie fidgeted, "and I'm sure having your nurse follow you home and constantly hover is enough to make anyone irritated."

"I reckon." Warrick nodded slowly. He sniffed at the air. "I don't smell no ham cooking. I'm hungry."

"You're always hungry."

"Only for you, Baby."

Natalie turned back around. With a laugh, Destiny ran at Warrick, jumping with a squeal, and he caught her, her legs going around his waist. Natalie kept her head down, busying herself with the sandwiches as the two disappeared. She heard them running up the stairs.

"Hey! Watch it, injured man coming through!"

Her spine stiffened at Martin's voice, followed by the occasional grunts, heavy footsteps, and a shower of sarcastic insults. She lowered the knife and focused on replacing the cap with the mustard.

"You not done with those sandwiches?"

She turned slowly, her eyes catching sight of Martin smiling in the doorway. Luke's tall form lingered behind him. She weakly shot a smile back, her eyes catching Luke's. He said nothing. After a moment, she cleared her throat and gestured at the sandwiches. "I wasn't sure what else besides mustard you might want on the bread."

Luke shoved harmlessly past Martin with a limp, and she watched under her eyelashes. He began to dig through his coat on the rack. She spotted the cigarettes in his hand while he put the coat back. Her mouth dropped open as she watched him stick a cigarette into his mouth. "What do you think you're doing?" She shot her eyes at Martin, and Luke pulled his lighter from his jeans pocket. "You're going to stand there and just let him start smoking again?"

Martin shrugged and moved towards the fridge. "He's a grown man, Baby. I can't tell him what to do."

"You're going to smoke?" She placed her hands on her hips and glared at Luke, her nervous anxiety replaced by surprised disappointment. "You've gone two months without one!"

"You're not my mother."

Martin noticeably stiffened, and he pulled back from the fridge. "Dude."

"Sorry."

She didn't fail to notice he only shot Martin an apologetic look. "Martin may not want to stand up to you about this, but I do." She stepped close to him, ripping the cigarette out of his mouth, and snapped it in half. "It's disgusting. It's bad for your health, and with your medication, I don't think it's entirely such a good idea to smoke or drink."

Luke growled down at her. "Don't do that again."

"What are you gonna do, Mr. Big Shot?"

He stepped closer to her, his eyes flashing hot with sudden anger. "Don't do that again."

"Guys, whoa." Martin stepped in between them, pushing each back on the shoulder gently. "What the Hell has gotten into you two?"

Luke stepped back more. He growled again, slinging the cigarettes, and the pack bounced harmlessly against the wall to fall to the floor. The kitchen was silent as he limped towards the dining room.

"I'm sorry, Martin." She looked at him nervously. "I get rather uptight about smoking." She turned back to the counter. "My father used to smoke cigars all the time, and he thought blowing the smoke in my face was funny."

He reached out to touch her face with his hand. "You two had me worried for a second. Thought you some private war going on I didn't know about."

She bit the inside of her mouth. "I don't think he likes me very much."

"Nonsense. You're like the little sister he never had, one that hovers around a lot with a bucket of pills."

"I don't think that's it."

"Well, what is it?"

She scrambled her brain for a quick answer. "It's more like wicked stepsister."

"Don't be ridiculous." He piled the sandwiches onto a plate. "Trust me, you guys spend some alone time together, and I promise you won't want to stop playing dolls with him. It'll do him good. He needs more friends."

Warrick and Destiny managed to untangle themselves to return to the table. Natalie sat nervously in her seat. It wasn't uncomfortable. As they sat down, Tony swung by to see Luke sitting next to Warrick and Destiny in front of her. Martin had insisted she sit between him and Luke.

It was amazing to see them together, the conversations picking up while they passed the bowls and plates. Natalie insisted on making more than sandwiches and added soup and random vegetables she found in their pantry. On days like this, she wished she could eat up her guilt or make it disappear by cooking more than humanly needed.

She took the sandwich plate from Martin, picked up one to place it on her plate, and handed it to Luke. He took it without looking at her, but the feeling of his fingers moving down hers when he accepted the plate made her eyes dart to his face. He didn't look up, taking a sandwich, and he passed the plate to Tony.

"Babe, you okay?"

Her head swung sharper than necessary towards Martin. "Yes, sorry. I got caught up thinking about something."

"I hope it's not about work. You have a full week off from that place."

Natalie shrugged nonchalantly. "I hope they're okay while I'm gone. That place can get hectic," she muttered, taking a vegetable bowl from him. She dipped out green beans and passed the bowl to Luke without looking at him, jerking her hand away quickly as she felt him grip the side. She picked up her fork and stabbed a green bean without remorse. She scolded herself for acting so immature. This wasn't her. What was this proving?

Someone cleared their throat, and she looked up to find Warrick watching her. He took a sip from his glass. Immediately, she looked down and placed the bean into her mouth. She shifted in her seat, feeling her leg brush Luke's cast. She forgot her newly sworn vow of silence. "Are you okay? I didn't mean to..."

"I'm fine. Pass me the corn."

"Since when did you start eating corn?" Warrick frowned. "You hate corn."

"Probably around the same time you started dating crazy chicks." Martin wiped his mouth, barely moving his head in time to duck the balled-up napkin from Destiny. He lifted the bowl to Natalie. "There you go, make Luke happy."

The bowl slipped from her fingers, crashing on the table, and Natalie shoved her chair back, grabbing her napkin. Martin and Destiny rose too, each patting at the small mess.

"I'm sorry. My fingers slipped." She patted at the table, lifting the bowl of corn. "Here, Luke, sorry." She shoved it at him without looking and let go when she felt him take it.

"It's no big deal." Martin shrugged. "Sit down. I'll get some more napkins."

He ventured into the kitchen, and she retook her seat. Destiny collected the soaked napkins and followed him. She cleared her throat and looked up at hearing Warrick's soft chuckle.

He watched her again, a small smile on his face, and his eyes darted between her and Luke. Slowly, he lifted his glass back up to his mouth.

Natalie directed her gaze down again, her plate suddenly more interesting than anything she had seen her entire life.

"Let's go."

"I ain't playing basketball, and there's no way Luke can play."

"Luke can cheer lead."

"You guys go ahead." Luke's voice rumbled from his seat on the couch. "I need to take some medication and nap."

Destiny snapped the dishrag on the counter beside Natalie and marched into the living room. Natalie continued to wash the dishes in the sink and listened to Destiny join in loudly to the conversation.

"Warrick, I remember us having a conversation about shopping. You promised!"

"Baby, I..."

"No! We're going, and that's final."

Martin chuckled. "Aw, Destiny wants to charge something else on Warrick's card. I'm so surprised. I'm sorry, but his credit cards are all maxed out."

"Shut the hell up, Martin." Destiny snapped. "I don't remember anyone ever asking your opinion on anything!"

Natalie shook her head and placed the now final dry dish on the rack on the counter. She dried her hands with the sink towel and turned towards the door to find Martin standing there.

"Hey."

She smiled and tossed the rag back on the counter. "Are you guys going out to play hockey?"

"Nah," he rolled his eyes. "Cruella de Vil has Warrick on a tight leash, so I'm going to go with Tony to see his kids. Wanna go?"

"Someone needs to look after your brother."

"I'm sure he'll be-"

"You did say you wanted me to get to know him better, didn't you?" She shrugged and slid her hands into her pockets. "No better time than this."

"You're right." Martin nodded and placed a kiss on her forehead. "We'll be back shortly."

"I'll be here."

It was quiet in the house except for the sound of the television playing in the living room. Natalie tapped her fingers on the kitchen table and glanced at the clock. The boys had only been gone for twenty minutes, and she hadn't heard a sound from Luke. It was getting close to time to take his medication, and she knew for a fact it was upstairs. She entered the living room to find him lying on the couch, remote in his hand. "It's time to take your medication."

He didn't shift his attention away from the television. "Okay, go get it."

"I don't think that's how you ask someone nicely to do you a favor."

He shrugged, still not looking at her. "Please get my medication for me before I fucking die. Thanks."

"Okay, that's enough." She marched around the couch, bending to tear the remote from his hand. She hit the off button, watching in satisfaction when the TV went black before she tossed the remote on the table. "It's time to end the pity party. You're being worse than children at the hospital."

"Give me the remote back, Natalie."

"Why? So, you can rot your brain more with that crap? There's nothing good on anyway."

"I said, give it back." He shoved himself on his elbows, his back against the couch cushions.

"Or what? You'll attack me with witty sarcasm?"

Luke was up on his feet faster than she thought possible. She was fully aware then that the coffee table was the only thing separating them. "I'll kiss that loud mouth of yours and shut you up for good."

Shocked, she took a step back at the seriousness of his voice. "Luke."

"Natalie?" He slowly edged around the table, keeping his eyes on hers.

"Stop right there." She pointed out at him. "This has gone too far."

"What has?" Luke paused on the other side of the coffee table. She debated between staying and bolting for the door. "I don't know if I'm sure what you're talking about."

Her hand shook. She lowered it quickly. "We can't do this. I'm dating your brother, and you're not yourself. The medication is..."

"We're not doing anything," he took another step forward, "yet."

"Last night was a mistake on my part." Natalie sputtered, backing up. "I let concern for you pass a line I shouldn't have crossed. You were dazed, heavily medicated, and had just come out of sleep. You didn't know what you were doing."

"That's bullshit, and you know it."

"No, it's not." She squeaked as he took more calm steps towards her, and she felt the firmness of the wall come in contact with her backside. "Luke, please…"

"Please, what?" He trapped her there, his left arm rising to cut off her exit, and the corner of the wall boxed her in from the left. He remained inches away, gazing at her with dark, playful eyes. "What is it, Natalie?"

"Don't." She felt the whisper slip from her lips without force. "Don't do this to me."

"You've done this to me." He reached out, bringing his free arm up so his fingers could play with the silky strands of her hair hanging around her shoulders. "I heard your voice, Natalie, and I knew you were waiting for me when I opened my eyes. Martin and Warrick don't understand our connection, but we have it. You know it." His fingers released her hair, hand hovering over the skin of her arm to allow his hand to the side of her face, fingers brushing the skin of her neck. "I know you feel it every time we're in the room together. Everyone sees it, but you refuse to because of Martin."

"Martin and I…"

His lips twisted in annoyance. "Tell me, after two months of being with Martin, have you slept with him? Have you done anything but heavy petting and the occasional kiss?" He chuckled and trailed a finger along her jaw. "He kisses you more on the face than anywhere on your body. Admit it."

"I can't hurt him," she whispered. "I won't."

"Then end it with him before you do. Martin's strong; he'll get over it and move on to the next girl. He always does. Trust me. He's not in love with you."

"Why are you saying these things to me? He's your brother."

"This doesn't change the fact that I love him." His gaze lowered, and he shifted his attention past her face, his fingers brushing against the top of her low-neck sweater. "It doesn't change how I feel about you."

Her breath caught in her throat as she felt him snap loose the top button with a flick of his thumb. She clawed at the wall, afraid any minute she'd slip, the sound of his breathing and the feeling of the warmth that radiated off him so close to her making her light-headed.

"It doesn't change how you feel about me."

"I don't-"

He shifted to cup her face with his hands. "You do." Swiftly, he covered her mouth with his own, drawing them close to where he flattened her comfortably against the wall. Her hands clutched at his black hoodie, and he deepened the kiss without resistance. He tilted her head to gain more access to her mouth, tongue sliding against hers, and he moaned against her mouth.

Natalie was lost, delicious shivers sparking down her spine, and her hands slipped under his hoodie. She gasped as he bit her lower lip, growling at the feeling of her fingernails scraping the muscles of his stomach. He pressed his hips into her, releasing her face to shove his hands under her shirt, hands cupping her breasts through the lacy texture of her bra.

Breathing hard, Luke tore his mouth from hers. He stared down at her, lust swirling in his dark orbs. "I want you upstairs in my room."

"Luke, we-"

"Natalie, for once, don't fight me on this." He squeezed her with both hands, slipping his fingers into the cups of her bra. Her hips jerked involuntarily, eyelids threatening to snap shut. "Don't make me beg."

"No." The rejection tore from her lips, and she threw out her arm to separate them. She shoved him away, hands shaking while she straightened her clothing. She was mortified as the tears began to stream down her face. "I need to get out of here."

"Go where?"

"Away from you." She started for the door, but he grabbed her arm, swinging her back to face him. "Luke, let go!"

"You're not walking away from me, Natalie."

"I said, let go of me!"

"What the fuck is going on here?"

Natalie twisted her arm free, almost falling into the wall, and her wide eyes swung to see Warrick standing in the kitchen doorway.

CHAPTER NINE

Warrick glared at them, the muscles in his jaw clenching, and his eyes flashed. "I said," he barked, stepping further into the living room, "What the fuck is going on?"

"Rick, you left the bags in the ..." Destiny's voice trailed off. She came up behind him, eyes scanning the three of them, and without another word, she shrank back into the kitchen.

"Nothing's..."

"We were...."

"Shut up." Warrick grabbed Natalie by the upper arm and snatched his brother's ear. Luke yelped in protest. He moved them towards the couch, pushing Luke down with a careful eye on his leg, and shoved Natalie beside him. He placed his hands on his hips, looking between them. "Spill it."

Crossing his arms, Luke glared at Warrick with a fire of determination in his eyes. "I don't think this concerns you, Brother."

Natalie rubbed her wrist. "There's nothing to be concerned with in the first place."

"You both are shitty liars." Warrick chuckled, the anger not lost in his voice. "I was there at lunch. I know what I saw. I've been seeing it since the hospital. If you two are bumping uglies..."

"We are not bumping anything!"

"Yeah, nice vocabulary skills, Rick," Luke chuckled. "It's called fucking, not bumping uglies."

"We are not doing those things." Natalie shoved away from the couch and pointed at Warrick. "Don't you dare touch me like that again."

Destiny reappeared in the doorway, biting at her lip nervously.

"Luke and I haven't slept together. We aren't planning to sleep together. How dare you accuse me of that? Look at him!"

"Hey!"

She flinched at his cry of objection but ignored him. "He's injured, he's heavily medicated, and he's at home under the same roof with us. I wouldn't betray Martin that way."

"Betray me in what way?"

Natalie slapped her forehead.

Martin entered the living room, glancing around in confusion as he jerked off his gloves. "I asked you guys a question."

"Yeah," Warrick crossed his arms, eyeing Natalie with a smug look. "He asked you a question, Girlie."

"I didn't come here to get attacked." Her voice betrayed her strong words when it quivered with uncertainty. "I came here... I don't know why I honestly came here. This was a mistake." She shook her head. "Excuse me, please."

She shoved past them, bounding up the steps, and was halfway up when Martin stopped her, grabbing her arm to stall her. He was frowning, eyebrows furrowed in that way that always let a person think they were about to get in trouble. She had no fear of him hurting her, but the brooding look on his face caused her to step back towards the wall.

"Tell me what's going on, Natalie. I come home to everyone shouting at each other, and you and Warrick squaring off like you're about to throw down. What did I interrupt exactly?"

She rubbed her face with her free hand. "I can't do this. I thought I could, but I can't." Natalie motioned at her arm he held in a tight grip. "Please release me."

"Do what?" He let go, but she knew if she moved, he'd only grab her again. "What can't you do?"

"I can't be here. I'm no longer Luke's nurse. I have no right to barge into your life anymore; it's only complicating things. I... I can't be your girlfriend anymore. I'm sorry."

"You're breaking up with me?"

"I'm sorry."

"What the fuck? Everything was fine this morning, and now you're fucking bailing ship?"

"Don't cuss at me, Martin."

"I'll cuss if I fucking want to, Natalie. You're an adult; don't act like you've never heard the words. You're breaking up with me for no reason, and you expect me just to let you go on your merry way?"

"Don't act like this is breaking your heart." She gathered all the courage she ever found in her body and straightened her back as tall as possible. "And don't act like this is the first time a girl has dumped you." She pushed away from the wall. "I'm leaving. We're done. End of story."

"This isn't a switch you turn off and on when you want to, Natalie!" Martin reached for her, but she flinched, bumping hard into the wall. It caused him to stop, eyebrows furrowing in anger and confusion. "We were fine up until I left you here alone with Luke."

She froze, eyes locked on his. She wished for nothing more than to sink into the wallpaper as a light of realization sank into his eyes.

"What'd he do?" Martin demanded hotly. "What'd he say to you?"

"He didn't-"

"Bullshit, stop protecting him all the fucking time. He's not some kid." This time, he ignored the flinching of her body and grabbed her arms. "Tell me. What did he do? Did he say something to you or do something you didn't like?"

She broke away from his arms, falling to the wall again. "I kissed him." She wiped at the tears that had begun to stream down her cheeks unnoticed. She twisted away from him. "I can't explain why it happened, but it did. I didn't stop it. That's why we're done, Martin. Because I'm not worthy of being in this house with you any longer."

She saw his body stiffen out of the corner of her eye and turned her head to see his eyes turn cold, his jaw muscles popping as he ground his teeth. "You're right. We are done." Martin whispered strongly. "I think it's time you left."

She turned without a moment's hesitation and bound up the steps. She flew into the room she once shared with him, gathering her things.

Martin was gone when she came back down, no one else meeting her eyes except Luke. He remained sitting on the couch with his face showing no emotion. He didn't remove his eyes from her until the front door shut firmly behind her.

One Year Later

"Dr. Hamilton to the front desk. Dr. Hamilton to the front desk. Code 7-11. Code 7-11."

Natalie sighed with a shake of her head and glanced up at her patient with a gentle smile. "I'm sorry, Mr. Vargus. I'm going to have to take that." She glanced towards the nurse on her right. "Nurse Shaver, would you mind finishing up here?"

"No problem, Doctor."

With a nod, she left the room, quick steps taking her to the nurse's station. She fixed Melissa with a curious gaze. "What is going on? We don't have a 7-11 emergency code."

"I know." Melissa pointed to her plastic cup, the gas station symbol displayed on the side. "Daniel Beckford's test results came back from the lab, and they're all positive."

Frowning, she took the file Melissa extended and flipped it open. "Every single test?"

"Afraid so."

"Has anyone called him?"

"We figured you'd like to do it since you're his doctor."

"I'll take care of it now." She walked off without another glance at Melissa, concentrating on the folder, until she entered her office.

The phone call lasted only twenty minutes. Daniel took the news that he had liver cancer better than his wife, excusing himself so that he could comfort her. She hung up the phone, staring at it for minutes in silence.

"It's always hard when you have to give bad news."

Natalie covered her mouth with her hand. Dr. Stewart closed the door behind him. "I know you're right, but it still gets me every time."

"Try dealing with it for twenty-five years. It's going to happen, Natalie. You can't save them all."

She straightened up in her chair. "What can I do for you, Thomas?"

"You have a visitor that's been waiting for an hour. Says he's not leaving until he speaks to you."

Her heart felt like it stopped. With a nod, she ran a quick hand over her hair. "Please show him into my office."

Thomas disappeared into the hall, and she stood up, smoothing her white regulation coat. He opened the door again, and she inhaled sharply when a familiar patient entered behind him.

"Mr. Drowser," she greeted the old man. "Let me guess, you ate peanut butter again?"

Thomas rolled his eyes, shutting the door quietly behind him.

The vending machine ate her change again. "Of all the days!" She dug into her pockets and found a crumpled dollar. This time, it took her money without hesitation and spit the bottle of flavored water down the shoot to the bottom.

She nodded at the people who greeted her in the hall and approached her office. Her mind was elsewhere. It had been foolish for her to think that Luke had been waiting to see her. She stayed out of the Ward family's way during their visits for his therapy sessions. Even though they were on different floors, she locked herself away in her office until his time was up.

A year had passed since she felt Luke's lips against hers and saw hurt in Martin's eyes. She'd done what she had to because, in the end, all you had was family. She returned to hers.

It didn't stop her from waking up crying at night. At first, she thought it to be nothing but guilt. After the third night in a row, she woke up with tears blurring her vision. Her mind, however, was clear, even if the image of his face lingered.

The hospital staff immediately noticed the change in her focus and attitude. The gentle smile and caring nature remained, but she became a woman possessed, taking double shifts whenever possible. She threw herself into extra classes at the university and medical program, earning her diploma and license for practice in the fastest time ever recorded at the hospital. She was the youngest doctor on the staff at twenty-three years old. Despite this, she refused to slow down.

At the news of her success and, no doubt, the increase in her paycheck, her mother seemed to forget their previous battle of words. She called daily, leaving messages on the machine when Natalie refused to answer. Amelia was divorced and working, much to her mother's disgust at the local mall. Her father's business had dipped due to the economy, and he turned back to alcohol to cure his ills. Natalie gave a sympathetic ear, but that was the extent of her kindness. She had no doubt her mother would find a way to survive. She always did, at any cost.

Natalie entered her office and paused in the doorway as her eyes caught sight of a masculine figure standing by her desk. His back was to her, the familiar leather jacket, and a black beanie on his head. She cleared her throat, shut the door, and made her way around her desk.

"Mr. Ward, I apologize. I didn't know you were waiting."

Martin continued to study the numerous plaques on her wall. "You've been busy."

"Way of the world, I'm afraid." She lowered the water bottle and took a seat. She motioned for him to do the same. She smiled, the expression not meeting her eyes. "What brings you to my office?"

She wasn't surprised when he didn't sit. He brought his eyes back to hers. "I'm wasting time while Luke finishes his session. He only has two more."

"I'm glad to hear that, Mr. Ward. The hospital and its staff are always happy to have a successful case."

"Why do you keep calling me Mr. Ward, Natalie? You know my name."

She dropped the smile from her face. "I'm on the clock." Natalie tapped at the top of the small clock near the edge of her desk. "It's the time for such formalities." She leaned back in her chair. "I hate to be short with you, Mr. Ward, but I do have patients I need to see. If there's something I can help you with, I'd be more than happy to-"

"You lied to me."

"Excuse me?"

"You lied to me that day. You told me you kissed Luke."

"I had-"

"He kissed you first. He told me everything. I knew he would eventually tell me the truth; he doesn't keep secrets well."

Natalie clutched her water bottle.

"He said you tried to stop him, that you were arguing with him when Warrick came back." He shrugged. "It happened a lot faster than I had anticipated."

"What do you mean?"

He moved to the wall to straighten one of her plaques with the tip of his finger. "I knew Luke had a soft spot for you since day one. Everyone could see it, but I didn't want to. I thought it was a crush, and you didn't seem to feel the same, so I chose to ignore it." He turned back to face her. "Bad call on my part."

Natalie shook her head. "That's all it was, Martin, a stupid crush. It happens sometimes with patients. They get connected to a doctor or nurse on a personal level. I'm sure Luke's moved on to bigger and better things. I know that I have."

He cocked an eyebrow at her. "I can see that." He jabbed his thumb over his shoulder. "I'm sure all these plaques and awards have really filled that void in your life."

"There is no void."

Martin shook his head and approached her desk. "You never were good at lying to me." He ignored the scared expression in her eyes as he reached out and took her chin in his hand. "It's okay to feel something for someone than as a doctor, Natalie." Just as quickly, he released her and stepped back. "God knows you of all people should be happy." He glanced down at his watch. "I need to get going before Luke thinks I bailed on his ass." He shot her one last look. "Remember what I said, Natalie."

"Goodbye, Mr. Ward. It was a pleasure to see you again."

"You too, Natalie."

She didn't move until the door shut after him. Natalie wiped the tears that had collected on the lashes of her eyes. Her shoulders began to shake, but she jerked back as the phone rang. She snatched it up from the receiver. "This is Dr. Hamilton." She wiped her face. "Okay, I'll be right there."

CHAPTER TEN

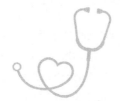

It took a week, but Natalie finally blocked the conversation with Martin from her mind by working double shifts. She ignored Melissa's concerned jabs and the nurses who fussed at her. A firm arched eyebrow and threat of an unpaid leave caused them to quiet down, but she found that was short-lived as they waited several hours before ganging up on her again.

Natalie slid the notebook into her desk and checked to ensure all the files had been piled carefully and neatly. She didn't look up when someone knocked on her open office door. "Yes?"

"There's a delivery for you at the front desk, Dr. Hamilton."

"Thank you, Laura. I'll be right there." She glanced up as the nurse turned to leave. "What is it?"

"It's a large package." Laura shrugged. "Melissa said you had to sign for it."

"Oh, okay," A racking cough halted her, and she placed a hand against her chest, leaning on the desk.

"Dr. Hamilton, are you okay?"

She cleared her throat. "I'm fine, thank you."

The nurse eyed her hesitantly. "I'll inform them you're on your way."

"Thank you." Natalie recollected herself, sipping her water bottle before heading to the nurse's station. Her mind scanned through the list of viable options of what could be waiting for her. She hadn't ordered anything recently, and no packages for the hospital had been billed in her name.

More than likely, Melissa was pulling another prank, and she again willingly fell for it.

Natalie continued down the hall. A passing nurse smiled, winking as she walked by her. Natalie frowned. Maybe she forgot that she-

She stopped several feet from the desk, eyes wide at seeing Luke standing there. He was leaning against the counter, laughing at Melissa while she chatted away. He was dressed in ripped jeans, a black shirt with different colored skulls covered by his black leather jacket. He said something that made Melissa laugh, and he smiled, the expression lighting up his entire face.

It was at that moment that he caught sight of her standing there. Luke moved away from the desk, hands at his sides as his eyes locked on hers. He moved forward at the same time she did, ignoring the people bustling around them and the eyes of several nurses, including Melissa, watching them.

Natalie stopped a foot away from him and tucked her hands into her lab coat pockets to keep them from shaking. "Mr. Ward, seeing you walking around again is good."

"Luke," he whispered. "I like it more when you call me by my name."

She shifted uneasily her feet and cleared her throat. "Luke, what brings you to my floor?"

"I finished my final session today." He scratched at the back of his neck. "I wanted to see you again before I left."

"Well, you've seen me."

He pursed his lips together. "I'm sorry about you and Martin. I told him what happened."

She paused, lifting a finger towards him to excuse herself, and coughed. She cleared her throat again as she turned back to face him. "I'm aware of that, Luke. Martin visited me about a week ago during one of your sessions."

"I hope things can work out with you two."

"There is no Martin and me, Luke." Natalie shook her head. "There never really was. I hope he's moved past whatever he thought he was feeling and found someone else."

"He tried, but it was impossible. What he thought was a crush ended up being something else instead."

"Why do I get the feeling you're not talking about Martin any-more?"

"Cause I'm not," Luke whispered. "I wanted to see you again." He glanced at his watch, "It's my last session, and I'm late for it."

She swayed slightly and lifted her hand to rub her temple. "I don't have time for this. I'm on a double, and I've got a ton of patients to get through before noon."

"I won't waste your time, but please, hear me out." Luke pleaded, taking a step towards her. "I was an idiot for acting so jealous over Martin, but I knew from the day I woke up and saw you holding my hand that I loved you. That feeling hasn't gone away. I've tried, and it just hasn't."

She kept her eyes down when he grabbed her wrists and placed her hands into his.

"I tried to forget you. I really did. As crazy as it sounds, you kept appearing in my dreams. I couldn't get you out of my head. I love you, Natalie."

"Luke, I..." She paused as another cough caught the end of her sentence, and her shoulders shook. She pressed her hand against her chest, and the coughing continued.

"Doctor Hamilton?" Melissa shoved back from her desk. Several nurses looked towards them at the sound of the woman's alarmed tone, a couple of them coming around the counter.

"Natalie, are you okay?"

"I'm fine." She waved her away, "Give me a minute to-" Her eyes rolled up in the back of her head, body crumpling, and Luke reacted instantly, catching her as she fell to the ground at his feet.

"Dr. Hamilton!"

"Code D, Doctor down! Code D!"

The beeping was loud next to her ear, but it became less noticeable as she felt the comfortable, warm sensation slowly crawling up her hand. With a groan, she regained consciousness and blinked against the bright lighting of the hospital room. She turned her head, her eyes meeting Luke's from where he sat beside her.

"Welcome back, Ms. Hamilton."

She smiled weakly. "This kind of looks familiar."

Luke chuckled. He reached out to stroke the side of her face. "Kind of." He smiled. "Dr. Stewart says you're going to be fine. He told me you haven't been taking care of yourself."

"You know me, I'm always looking out for everyone but myself."

"That's why you need someone to do it for you."

"That's what I've been telling her," Dr. Stewart strode into the room. He glanced down at his clipboard before focusing on Natalie with a look of simmered annoyance. The look disappeared as he saw her fully awake, and he smiled, making him seem human once again. "Glad to see you back with us, Natalie."

"Glad to be back, Thomas." Natalie waved with her free hand weakly. "So, what's the story, Doc? How long do I have?" She winced as Luke squeezed her hand and shot him an apologetic smile. "Just a joke."

"Not funny," he grumbled.

"I second that." Dr. Stewart shoved his folder under his arm. "Seems you have a case of the flu."

"Give me some time, and I'll be back on the floor in a week."

"I know, that's why I'm suspending you for three."

"What?" She tried to sit up, but her head spun out of control. She fell weakly against the pillows. "Are you crazy?"

"I told you if you ran yourself down, there'd be consequences. You'll be paid for the days of excused absences." Thomas glanced over at Luke before returning his attention to her. "I sincerely hope you have someone to look after you while you recover."

"She does," Luke spoke up. "A whole family of people."

"Now, wait a –"

"Good." Thomas shook his head at her. "This isn't open for discussion. Prescriptions are waiting for you at the front desk and papers you must sign before you leave. I suggest you take this vacation seriously and regroup." He glanced over his shoulder. "I think you have some people here to see you."

Natalie looked over to see Warrick and Destiny, Martin in the background with Anthony and his family in tow. They surrounded the bed, their hands full of flowers and balloons.

"We thought you could use some cheering up."

She smiled, blinking away tears as she felt Luke squeeze her hand. "I don't know what to say."

"How about thank you?" Martin grinned. He waved around a pink Get Well balloon. "This cost me a couple of well-earned dollars and a few macho points with your hot nurses."

With a short laugh, she nodded. "Thank you."

He winked. "No problem."

"What do you say we get out of here?" Destiny patted the bed. "I'll make some special soup for you."

"We're trying to get her well again, not kill her."

Destiny rolled her eyes but grinned down at Natalie. "Let's give her a moment to get dressed." She shoved Warrick out of the room, the rest of the group following.

Martin cleared his throat, placing flowers and the balloon on the tray beside her bed. "We'll wait for you at the front desk."

"Thank you."

Martin ducked out of the room and shut the door behind him. She cleared her throat, glancing down to find her hand still in Luke's.

"Does this mean you love me too?"

Her eyes found his.

"You don't have to say anything." With a smile, he raised her hand. He pressed a soft kiss on the palm of her hand. "I already know the answer to that question." He rose from his seat. "I'll give you a few minutes to yourself. I'll wait outside your door."

She nodded, watching him walk to the door and swung it open. "Luke?"

He hesitated with a look over his shoulder. "Yes?"

"I love you."

He grinned. "I know."

She laid back against the bed pillows, smiling as the door shut behind him. She looked towards the windowsill and spotted the vase of wildflowers. Her fingers touched something on the bed, and she glanced down to see Luke had placed a single wildflower beside her hand.

It was the most beautiful thing she had ever seen.

CHAPTER ELEVEN

N atalie glanced around Luke's room, cluttered with boxes, and let out a long sigh.

"What's wrong?" He asked where he sat on the bed with a pen and paper in hand.

"I have too many things."

"You gave away three-quarters of your stuff when you decided to move in." He abandoned his notebook and moved off the bed. He moved stiffly, but she saw improvement with each day that passed. He crouched down next to her and studied the boxes. "Everything will fit." He pressed his lips against her hair. "Why don't we get started, and we'll figure it out as we go?"

"I've got to go to work." The six weeks off for recovery ended two days ago. Today was her first official complete shift back. She looked over at Luke. "I don't want to go to work."

Once upon a time, the hospital made up for everything her personal life lacked and gave her a sense of purpose. Now she'd realized that there was more than helping others get well; there was also living a life of her own. Luke helped her know she wanted more; his family made her realize that family wasn't determined by blood alone. She was now part of the Ward family and treated as if she'd always been.

Her childhood hadn't prepared her for what a real family meant. The only unconditional love she'd received was from a woman paid for her services. She realized things didn't always run smoothly in a real family. There were more likely to be fights in the Ward house than hugs, but love and acceptance shone through, even during the most vicious of battles.

Luke stroked her hair. "You should tell them that you need more time off."

"I've taken off more time than I can afford." She left the rest of her thoughts unspoken, that continued time off was more than they could afford because it would only upset Luke. Since his injuries, he was working again, but he couldn't do the same physical labor he'd been used to before it.

"You're only working one shift, right?"

"I'm working my standard eight-hour shift."

"While you're at work, I'll see what I can do about making your stuff fit."

"Luke, I can do it."

"I can help you. I don't have to be at work for a few hours, and the paperwork will only take me an hour. Don't argue with a Ward, Hamilton; you'll never win."

"I will win eventually." Natalie rose to her feet and dusted her hands off. "I need to shower and change into my scrubs."

"Are you annoyed that they transferred you to the ER to the trauma floor?"

It wasn't that she didn't like the new position, but a part of her wondered if she'd received the transfer, not because she was qualified for the job, but because Doctor Stewart thought she couldn't handle her floor any longer.

"You okay?"

She moved to the closet and grabbed a pair of candy pink scrubs. "I'll be fine." She cleared her throat, "I think Destiny said she was cooking tonight, but if she's not in the mood..."

"I'll cook something." Luke sat down on the bed to watch her. "What time is your lunch break? I can visit you."

"I'm not sure. I'll grab something from the vending machine when I can." He made a snorting sound, and she looked over at him. "What?"

"You're so skinny you'll break if the wind is strong. You need more than something from a machine." He remembered clearly how she'd been nothing but skin and bones several weeks ago. Dr. Stewart said it was part of why the flu hit her so hard.

He could hear his mother's voice in his mind. Eleanor would have taken extreme pride in nursing Natalie back to health. It hit him, as it always did when he thought of her, how much he missed her and how days never passed that he didn't wish she were still with them. She would have approved of him and Natalie. He frowned, lost for a moment in his thoughts. Ma would have worried about Martin. Over the past year, he hoped from woman to woman like it was a competitive sport. A good-natured bet was between himself, Tony, and Warrick if Martin would catch something or have a kid first. With each faceless woman, the pot rose.

"I'll get something from the cafeteria." Natalie amended. She glanced down at her watch. "I am going to be so late. I've got to get in the shower."

"Want company?" He questioned to watch her face flush. She may have moved into his bed, but they weren't intimate. It was a fact that caused him to take huge loads of shit from his brothers, but the teasing was all in fun.

"You wouldn't know what to do if I said yes." She retorted primly as she clutched her scrubs to her chest. He could see the worry that popped into her eyes. Her words might have been light-hearted, but he knew she thought she expected more than she gave him.

"You're going to be late. Make sure that you call me when you're going to take lunch." He added. "I'm going to head into the office for a bit. I'll come home later and tackle these boxes."

Several hours passed in the blink of an eye. Natalie stopped for two minutes to chow down a protein bar and guzzle a bottle of water when the pager on her hip went off. She swallowed hastily and reached for the house phone. She dialed the department number that had popped up on the tiny screen. "This is Doctor Hamilton. I was paged?"

"This is Trina in the ER. I've got a MVA incoming, pregnant female passenger, and was severely injured. We've got an ETA of four minutes."

"I'll be there in two." Natalie tossed the rest of her food into the trash, the plastic bottle into the recycle bin, and avoided the elevator. She took the stairs, her only exercise these days; she'd slacked off on running because she'd rather spend time in bed with Luke.

She arrived at the emergency room and was pointed towards Trina. The nurse offered a grim smile. "The EMT's called in. Her pressure is dropping, and she's bleeding from a laceration close to her femoral artery. They can no longer get a pulse on the fetal monitor."

"How far along is she?"

"Seven months."

"Call upstairs and have an OR prepped. We're going to need to move quickly. Losing them is not an acceptable option for me."

The nurse met her eyes and nodded. "It's not an option for me either."

The patient's husband had been killed in the wreck. The good news was that the mother and baby were expected to recover fully. With a sigh, Natalie opened a fresh bottle of water and took a long sip from where she rested against the wall of the NICU.

"Impressive work today, Doctor Hamilton."

She looked up to see Dr. Stewart's familiar face. "Thank you."

"You're halfway through your shift. That's typically the time that you would take lunch." He glanced down at her scrubs. "You might want to think about changing your clothes as well."

It was only then that she noticed the blood on her. "I'll do that right away."

"Perhaps you'll meet me in the cafeteria when you're done. We never did get a chance to celebrate your promotion. Be assured, Natalie, this was a promotion. You needed a change from the trauma unit."

"I was perfectly capable of continuing to work on the trauma floor. My work was impeccable. I spent more hours there than..."

He held up a finger. "That is precisely why I determined you needed to be transferred. Sometimes, I wasn't even sure you had an apartment to call home. I suspected that you were living out of your locker. You're an excellent doctor; you've proved that time and time again. You're willing to work yourself to the bone, and you did that. You pushed yourself too far. If I hadn't decided to transfer you, I don't believe you'd be here right now."

"With all due respect, Doctor Stewart, that's ridiculous. Dedication is not a flaw. I've dedicated years of my life to my profession, to this hospital, and to be dismissed from a more challenging position is an insult." Natalie held her head up high. "I'd like to take this chance to request a transfer back to the trauma floor officially."

"That is a request I cannot grant as easily as snapping my fingers. Dr. Miller is now in charge of the trauma ward...."

She cut him off. "If I am not reinstated to my previous position, I will be forced to offer my resignation and seek counsel from a lawyer for sexual discrimination. Would it be an issue if a male doctor spent as many hours as I did there?"

"I don't like your tone. It's an issue for me when any doctor on my staff appears to be on a path to self-destruction." Dr. Stewart kept his voice low. "Your threat of resigning isn't going to force my hand and have me transfer you back. That's the end of the story. I suggest you change, and take a break to clear your head."

Natalie shoved past the man she'd always looked to as a mentor and father figure. She took the stairs and headed for the roof. The Pittsburgh air was bitter with cold and the scent of diesel fuel from the trucks. She stood near the edge and looked down, unsure if she should start laughing or crying.

He thought that she was going to fall apart. It was ridiculous. There was nothing left to fall apart; if anything, her dedication to her job kept her from losing her mind. She stepped back and sat down on the cold concrete with a sigh.

Her job was all she had before she met Luke. The thought of him brought a smile to her face, and she nearly reached into her pocket for her phone. She knew that if she called him, he'd come to the hospital, and nothing good would come from that. He'd be angry that Doctor Stewart had upset her. That could end badly.

Rethinking her approach, she took out her phone and dialed the office number. Luke said he had paperwork to do. He liked to dawdle over it as if the figures and forms would work themselves out.

Martin answered gruffly after a few rings. "Yeah?"

"That's how you answer the phone at work?"

"Shit, it's only you, Tinkerbell. Your boyfriend isn't here if that's why you're calling. No one is but me, and I'm about to throw this computer through the fucking window. Why do I need a password and a username?"

"Your username is Martin, and your password is Martin." Natalie smiled at the silence that followed.

"Well, I guess I should have thought of that." He cleared his throat. "Like I said, Luke isn't here. He took off with Destiny about an hour ago."

"Where did they go?"

"Hell, if I know, I didn't ask. I was just glad to get rid of Destiny. That woman does not have a damn off switch. Are you at the house?"

"I'm still at work. I was taking a break. I had a rough first part of my shift."

"Did someone mess with you?" She could hear his chair scraping against the floor. "Do I have to fuck someone up? I could use the distraction."

"What's wrong?"

"It's my turn to do the books."

"If you bring them back to the house, I'll do them when I get home." Most months, she ended up doing them anyway. Luke hated numbers, Tony and Warrick were always too distracted, and Martin blew up because the business continued to operate in the red.

"You're not a magician, Tinkerbell. There's nothing that you can do that I can't."

Guilt sparked in her stomach. Her savings were meager at best. She rose to her feet and glanced out at the skyline. Seeing Hamilton Tower lit up in the distance was an insult to injury. How often had her father pointed out the building and told her it was her legacy? Now, it was nothing. The day she'd chosen to refuse to participate in the cotillion that her mother painstakingly planned was when she'd been informed her inheritance hinged on her doing what her parents felt was best for her.

They tolerated all her years of volunteering at the hospital because it would look good on her college applications. Her purpose in life was to go to college to find a man to marry. That was Veronica Hamilton's dream. It damn sure hadn't been hers.

"Tinkerbell? Did I lose you?"

"I'm here, Martin. I'm going to head back in and finish my shift." She consulted her watch again. "I've got four more hours."

"Did you eat?"

"Yes." A protein bar was considered food. "Hey, out of curiosity, how much money do we need to break even this month?"

"Uh, wait a second." She heard him shuffling papers around. "It's about ten grand. We got stiffed on that rehab job we did on Jones Street, and we can't put off paying the lumber yard any longer. They already gave us ninety-day terms." He paused. "Why do you ask?"

She focused on her watch. "No reason."

"Don't worry about it. Get back to work. I'll tell Luke you called if I see him."

Easier said than done.

CHAPTER TWELVE

"M s. Hamilton, are you certain you wish to part with this piece? It is a classic design that will indefinitely be in style."

She smiled at the man and signed the receipt. "Mr. Jones, you've tried to talk me out of this for an hour. I've made up my mind. Now, if you can't meet my price..."

"I'm stealing this watch from you. Twelve thousand dollars is..."

"Twelve thousand is all that I'm asking from you."

"I can't transfer to your account until the morning." The elderly man frowned, "Dear, if you're in trouble financially, you might want to call your parents."

That was the problem with dealing with any high-end jeweler in Pittsburgh. Her mother was fond of sparkly baubles, and her father catered to her in every way possible. "Tomorrow morning is fine."

"I could give you some cash, but I don't keep much in the store."

"Again, the morning will be fine, Mr. Jones." Natalie rose to her feet. "However, one item in your case caught my eye."

The smell of spicy Spanish food filled the air when she entered the house. Natalie slid her coat from her shoulders in the warmth of the entryway. She kicked off her sneakers, her feet feeling instant relief as she slipped them into the slippers she kept by the door. She fingered the box in her scrub top pocket and followed the sound of voices to the dining room.

"Nat's home! We can finally eat." From his seat at the table, Warrick grabbed for a plate. Destiny swiftly swatted his hand with a serving spoon. "Ouch!"

"Let her sit down, Rick. Have some manners."

Luke smiled. "We realized that we never celebrated your promotion, so..." He motioned to the table. "We're all proud of you."

"We're all starving too," Warrick added.

Luke turned to glare at his brother. "This is an important night for Natalie. You could at least act like you care."

She knew the signs of a Ward argument about to break out, so she cleared her throat and sat down beside Luke. "It smells delicious. I agree with Rick. Let's eat."

Destiny began to dish out the food. The men couldn't argue with their mouths full, and the meal passed peacefully. She ate like she was starving and ignored how Luke looked at her. She should have slowed down. Her hunger made it obvious she hadn't eaten during the day.

Martin threw down his napkin onto the table. "Well, Kids, this has been fun, but I've got shit to do."

"Don't you mean some random hooker from Ace's Bar?" Destiny questioned.

"I don't pay for it, Cruella, unlike some people here." He shot a glance over at Warrick as Destiny flipped him the bird and followed Warrick into the kitchen. "Sometimes she is too easy."

"Sometimes you're too mean, Martin. You know she will scream at him all night for not defending her." Natalie shook her head. "You really shouldn't refer to a date as having shit to do."

"I never said it was a date, Tinkerbell." He winked at her. "I left the bills we were talking about upstairs in your room. You might as well toss the ones we couldn't pay. No fucking point in staring at them."

"I'll take care of it."

"Take care of Luke first. His balls have to be navy blue by now."

"Fuck you, Martin."

"At least I get fucked," Martin chuckled. "I'm out of here. See you guys in the morning."

"Don't catch anything."

In response, the older brother flipped up his middle finger and left the dining room. Natalie shook her head with a soft smile. "He's looking to find someone, Luke. He's got to be lonely."

"He's only looking to get laid."

"It can't be easy for him being surrounded by couples. He's got to feel left out."

"Sweetheart, you're cute. Trust me, he wants to get laid."

"Is that why he pursued me?"

"That was different. You're not like the girls he's after now. You're a good girl."

"Don't patronize me, Ward."

"I'm not patronizing you. I'm saying if Martin wanted a relationship after the two of you stopped whatever it was, he'd be dating a different class of woman right now. He'd be dating women who wanted to date."

"Maybe he doesn't want to say he's looking for someone?" She stood up from the table. "Either way, I don't want to spend tonight talking about Martin."

Luke grinned and reached out for her. "Oh yes, Babe? What do you want to do?"

"I saw something today and thought that you'd like it." She reached into the pocket of her scrubs. Even though she felt slightly self-conscious, the look of apprehension on his face was not helping, so she extended the box to him. "Take it, Luke. It doesn't bite."

"Natalie, you didn't have to buy me anything. I know that money is tight for you and-"

"Don't say anything, take it." When he didn't immediately take the box, she set it down on the table, hurt clearly in her eyes. "I'm going to see if Warrick needs help with the dishes."

"Wait. I'm serious. You didn't have to buy me anything."

"No shit, Luke." It was so rare when she cursed that his eyes went wide with surprise. "I bought it because I wanted to get you something nice. If you don't want it, leave it sitting there."

She turned on her heels and stormed into the kitchen, only to find Destiny and Warrick doing things that Martin hadn't intended when he'd installed the new kitchen counter. "Shit, I'm not looking. Sorry." She whirled around and smacked into Luke. A frustrated grunt escaped her lips, and she shoved past him.

"Natalie, please don't walk away from me."

The box was still sitting on the table. The sight of it angered her. She should have held it in, counted to ten, and let it go. Either she'd spent too much time around the Ward family, or she'd finally reached her quota for bullshit after the day. She whirled around when Luke called her name again. "I buy you a gift, and you act like I gave you crabs! The sex kind of crabs, not the tasty ones that you can eat!"

Warrick let out a bark of laughter from the kitchen. "Shut up, Rick! Don't you have better things to do with your mouth? Don't smirk at me, Luke Ward, because do you know what?

You are not cute, not at all."

"Natalie..."

"Don't say my name all sweet. You buy me things all the time! You randomly come home with books or flowers, but I buy you something, and you don't have the decency even to open the damn box?"

"I know that it's hard for you financially right now. That's all that I was trying to say." He took several steps forward. "I don't want to fight with you."

"Well, that's too bad!" She stomped her slipper-clad foot and propped her hands on her hips in a stance that instantly reminded him of Destiny. "We're fighting, and you're not getting around it."

"I don't want you to spend all your money on me!"

"I didn't."

"I love you, Natalie."

"That's not going to fix this. I bought you that trinket because I thought that you'd like it. I figured it would make you smile, but you haven't even looked at it." Natalie felt tears well in her eyes. "Martin won't be home tonight, so I'm going to crash in his room."

"You are not sleeping in Martin's bed. He's likely to stumble home drunk in the middle of the night and think that you're one of his floozies."

"Well, at least I'd get touched." She had venom in her voice that Luke never heard. "Don't look at me like that, it's true. I'm such a good girl that you won't even touch me sometimes. I try, and you..."

Warrick let out another hoot of laughter. "Shut up, Warrick." Destiny's voice carried clearly.

Luke's nostrils flared. "You've been sick and weak. You need to get better, and me pawing you at any given opportunity isn't how to make that happen."

"I'm not weak, but don't worry, I won't ever expect you to attempt to paw me again." She ran her hands through her hair.

"You're being completely unreasonable."

"You want to see unreasonable? I'll show you fucking unreasonable!" She stalked over to the table and grabbed the box. She launched it at him, but he caught it quickly before the box reached the intended target of his head. With a frustrated growl, Natalie considered throwing the salt and pepper shaker left behind on the table.

"Would you calm down?"

"I left calm a few stops back." Natalie stormed past him without waiting for his response. She made her way up the stairs and down the hall to Martin's bedroom, slamming the door with a thud. She exhaled as she looked around the room. Not much had changed since she'd spent her nights there. His things were still mingled with Eleanor's as if he couldn't let go of his mother. She stepped forward to run her fingers over the rosary that hung from the mirror.

With a sigh, she flopped down on the bed, letting out a short, frustrated scream into one of the pillows. This was precisely why she'd been better off before getting sick. Her job didn't fight with her. It didn't piss her off. It allowed her to focus and keep her mind filled with thoughts not about her life.

She didn't enjoy thinking about herself. A psychiatrist would have a field day with that fact, but she'd never seen any benefit in therapy. She knew that her parents did a number on her. Not living up to their expectations gave her a sense of failure even though she'd done nothing but succeed. Her failed and painful brush with a grown-up relationship left her disappointed and, once again, doubting herself.

Six weeks ago, her life was simpler, even if she had nothing resembling a social life. Natalie turned to her side and wrinkled her nose at the stench of Martin's sheets. "Ugh." She swung her feet off the bed and began to tug off the blanket and sheets. When was the last time, if ever, they'd seen the inside of the washing machine?

She was pulling the pillowcases off when Luke shoved open the door. "What are you doing?"

"I refuse to sleep on stinky sheets. I'm going to wash these and put on fresh ones from the linen closet." She tugged at the last corner of the sheet. "What do you want?"

"I don't want to fight with you." He stepped forward. "I want you to look at me while I open your present."

"Oh, now you want it?" She snorted and gathered the dirty sheets in her arms. "Enjoy it. I've got laundry to do if Destiny and Warrick aren't testing the spin cycle again."

He blocked her exit. "I'm sorry that we fought. I don't want to fight with you." He sighed. "Before Martin and I came to live with Eleanor, all my foster parents did was argue. I couldn't sleep at night because they fought so much. I don't want that for our relationship."

"Maybe we shouldn't have a relationship, Luke."

"What?"

"We rushed into this. If I hadn't passed out that day, you would have gone on your way, and I'd have continued mine." Natalie dropped the sheets onto the floor. "That would have probably been the best for both of us."

He moved forward and grabbed her arms. "Don't ever say that again."

"What am I supposed to say? It was a stupid present, and now we're at each other's throats." She could only imagine the reaction when she took the remaining eleven thousand eight hundred dollars and used it to pay off the family's outstanding bills. For the first time in a year, they'd end the month in the black, and she'd been so excited for it. Now, she felt hollow inside.

"I'm not used to people buying me things, for anyone to see something and think of me. The only other person who did that was Mom. I overreacted. I fucked up." She watched as his face grew tight, and he dropped his hands from her arm. "I'm sorry, Natalie."

She stepped close to wrap her arms around him. "I don't like to fight with you either. I might have taken things too far, but it didn't seem like you wanted it, and it doesn't seem like you want me, and I..."

"I love you, Natalie. I'll always want you."

"If you don't like it, we can take it back."

"Let me take a look at it, Sweetheart." He shifted his hand to reach into his pocket. He drew out the black box and quickly opened it to reveal the bracelet. "It's beautiful. I love it. I love you." He pressed a kiss to her forehead.

"Was that so hard?" She sniffled. "That's all that you had to do downstairs."

"It has skulls on it."

"You like skulls. You've got them on most of your shirts."

"Yeah, I guess I do." He wrapped his arms around her again. "What do you say we leave Martin's nasty sheets here and head to our room?

You look tired." He pulled back to stroke her hair. "Was it a bad day at work?"

"There was a bad accident, and we almost lost the mother and her baby," she sighed. "I fought with Doctor Stewart and demanded to be returned to the trauma floor. I threatened to resign if he didn't reassign me."

"You're just now telling me this?"

"We were busy fighting. It was the last thing on my mind." She shut her eyes to inhale the scent of him. "Luke Ward, have you been smoking?"

"I might have had one right before you came home."

"It's a dirty habit."

"I know. I'm sorry."

She tilted her head back. "Does that offer for you to join me in the shower still available?"

Luke made a sound like he was choking. "Yeah, it's still good."

She smirked. "Good to know. I was checking."

"Oh, that's cruel." He leaned down so that he could kiss her lips lightly. "If I remember correctly, I lost all privileges to paw you."

"Let's see what we can do to get those privileges back." She let her eyes meet his. "We'll start with the shower."

Steam filled the bathroom. Natalie sighed as Luke ran her bath sponge down her back. He'd already washed and conditioned her hair. He was working up a soapy lather with the sponge, making her body temperature rise with his careful attention to detail. Several times, she'd tried to turn the shower from a necessary function to a fun time. He responded to her touches but limited the encounter to a heated make-out session. Frustration built inside of her, and she huffed loudly.

He let out a low chuckle. "I'm not making love to you for the first time in the shower."

"Turn off the water, and let's head to bed."

He smiled, and it dazzled her as much as his kisses. "I want it to be special."

"You act like it's my first time, Luke."

"You've told me that you've had sex, and you came away from it hurt. That's not going to happen this time. We decided to take it slow. We're going to take it slow."

"When did we decide that?" She pouted.

He twisted the knobs to turn the water off. "We decided that when I realized that you'd never had an orgasm before now." He pushed the curtain back and motioned for her to join him as he grabbed a towel. She did, a slight blush covering her cheeks. He wrapped the soft fabric around her. "Did you leave your lotion in the bedroom?"

"Are you putting my lotion on for me?"

"I'll do anything for you, Sweetheart."

CHAPTER THIRTEEN

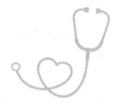

S he was late for work. Her business at the bank took longer than she'd expected. The transfer arrived, and she'd taken immense pleasure in depositing the money from her account to the Ward business account. She'd neatly written out the necessary checks, sealed the envelopes, and done a joyful shimmy as she dropped them into the mailbox. They'd be in the black this month, to hell with whatever repercussions would come her way.

She glanced down at her wrist; the simple silver watch there now suited her better than the Rolex had. Her parents presented it to her on the day she graduated from high school, and if she suspected she might miss it, she would have been wrong. The peace of mind of knowing that the company was secure meant more than the trinket her parents had tossed at her like a treat to a well-behaved pet.

When she arrived at the hospital, she knew it was time to eat some crow. Her outburst at Doctor Stewart had been inappropriate. She'd realized after getting a whole night of sleep and talking to Luke a little more. She'd been on the verge of a breakdown, her collapse evidence of that. She found Doctor Stewart in his office with a coffee cup in hand. "I know you're very busy, but I wanted to apologize for..."

"There's no need for apologies, Natalie. I didn't expect any different reaction from you. My wife gave me an earful last night about my inability to talk to women."

"You were honest. That counts for something. I just wasn't ready to hear it." Natalie cleared her throat and sat in the seat before his desk. "My threat of resignation was spoken out of anger. I love this hospital, and I don't want to leave."

"That's good because I'm not granting your request. Now, get to work."

She was exhausted when she found ten minutes to take for herself. She sat in the employee lounge, pulled out her cell phone, and saw that she missed several calls. A quick check told her she'd hit the phone onto the vibrate option. With a sigh, she dialed the number back.

"Ward Brothers Construction." Anthony's pleasant voice greeted her.

"Hey Tony, it's Natalie. I saw that someone called me a few times."

"Girl, we all called you." She heard him cover the phone and holler for his brothers. She was greeted with all the Wards talking at once through the modern marvel of a multi-line office phone system. The comments ranged from a hello from Luke to curses from Martin, followed by Warrick's laughter.

"I can't understand if you all talk at once."

"What the fuck did you do?"

"Calm down, Martin," Anthony interjected. "Nat, I called the bank to negotiate a short-term loan to cover the money that we were short, and imagine my surprise when the manager told me that there had been a large deposit from your account this morning."

"I came into some money."

"You came into some money? That's finding twenty fucking dollars on the street. The checks that were written out of the account were..."

Natalie silenced Martin's voice in the only way she could. She ended the call and powered down the phone. Perhaps she could negotiate to pull a double shift. Hopefully, the rational Ward, Anthony, would keep the others from visiting the hospital. She didn't want her business out in the open for everyone. There was no shortage of people who knew she was one of the Hamiltons. The Carters were the only family holding more power in the city.

She pushed away all of her thoughts and rose to her feet. It was time to get back to work.

With a sigh, Natalie brought her car to a stop in front of the house. Anthony's truck was next to Martin's Buick. There was no point in putting off the inevitable. She barely reached the front door when it swung open to reveal Martin. His jaw was set in a hard line as he frowned at her. "What the Hell did you do? How did you get that kind of money, Nat?"

It had been so long since he'd called her anything but Tinkerbell that she knew she was in a world of shit. "Can I get my coat off before we start the argument part of this evening's entertainment?"

"This isn't a joke. What did you do? You don't come into that much money out of the blue! You were checking the couch for change to get a soda for work the other day!"

She weighed her options and decided to go with the truth. It would come out anyway. She might as well say it. "I sold my watch."

Martin let out a snorting sound. "No one was going to pay you that much for your knockoff Rolex."

"It wasn't a knockoff."

Appearing behind Martin, Luke cleared his throat. "You shouldn't have done that, Natalie."

"It was my watch, and we needed the money." Stepping into the house and shutting the door, she took her time slipping off her jacket and hanging it up. "Would you all stop staring at me, please?"

"Where did you get a real Rolex? You know what? It doesn't even matter. We stopped payment on the checks." Martin reached into his pocket and thrust a piece of paper at her. "This is a check for the amount."

"Why would you do that?!" Natalie demanded. "Those bills needed to be paid."

"Those bills aren't your problem," Martin told her bluntly. He turned and handed the check over to Luke. "Make sure that she cashes it, or I'm going to put a hurting on you."

"Luke doesn't control what I do!"

"Make sure that she deposits the check, Luke."

Anthony shook his head and stood up from the couch. "Natalie, it was incredibly sweet of you to want to help us, but the bills aren't yours. They're ours, and Wards always pay their debts."

"But that's what I did! We needed the money. My watch was a meaningless trinket."

"You call that a trinket?" Martin snorted. "I forget sometimes that you're a rich girl."

"I am not rich," she snapped. "As you pointed out earlier, I was searching the couch for change the other day." Her eyes focused on him. "I did what I wanted to do with that money, and stopping the checks isn't going to keep me from doing it. I'll write the check out of my account; it's as simple as that."

"No, you're going to return to whatever pawn shop has your watch and get it. That's the end of the discussion." Martin growled. "We'll pay our debts; that's what Wards do."

"I'm not a Ward? That's funny because, since the day you all brought me home from the hospital, you told me that's what I am. You told me that I'm family, but now, when it comes down to it, I'm suddenly not family anymore?"

"That money is not paying our bills, and I've got things to do, so this conversation is over. Cash the fucking check, get your watch back, and from here on out, you're not going to have any access to the business account."

"Martin!" Luke and Anthony spoke at the same time. Warrick shook his head when her mouth dropped open.

Natalie blinked. Hurt rolled through her like a wave. She grabbed the check from Luke's hand and ripped it into several small pieces. She tossed the paper in the air, and the pieces fluttered to the ground. "I'm going to overlook that you never think before you speak, Martin."

Luke frowned. "We never discussed removing her access, Martin. Natalie's been a huge help with the business."

"Luke, everything is fine. I know where I stand now." Natalie cleared her throat. She turned her attention to Anthony. "I have no intention of taking the money back. You were looking for a loan, and I'm offering you one without interest or the need for repayment. If you don't take the money from me directly, I will still find a way to pay them." Her eyes went back to Martin's. "Even if I'm not family, Ward Brothers Construction matters to me."

"Your offer is generous," Anthony rose to his feet, "and while you're definitely a Ward," He added quickly, "I don't feel right taking your money. None of us do."

"Luke, is that true?"

"It's a lot of money, Babe; money you could use for your student loans. I know most of your paycheck goes towards that and the charities you support." He stuck his hands in his pockets.

"Do I need to explain the reality of the company going without funds?" She demanded, "Or is it impossible for me to care about that because I'm not a Ward?" Even saying the words caused an ache in her chest that had no physical cause. Emotional pain felt just as sharp. "Now we're done with the conversation because I've said everything I have to say." She ignored everyone and moved up the stairs.

Immediately, Luke followed her. "Natalie, wait."

"If you don't want to fight, don't even mention what happened down there."

He followed her into their bedroom and shut the door. "I don't want to fight."

She gasped and looked around the room. Her things were unpacked and mixed with his. The twin bed he'd slept on since childhood was gone and replaced by a full-sized bed. The comforter set was new, a dark chocolate brown with bright fuchsia flowers spattered over it. "Destiny helped me pick it out. She said you might feel like this wasn't your home."

Without a word, she turned to hug him, and he wrapped his arms around her as she sniffled.

"Please don't cry, Baby."

"I wanted to do something nice for everyone. I wanted to help!"

"Honey, it was over ten thousand dollars."

"Do you think of me as a Ward, Luke?"

"I do."

"If that's true, it doesn't matter if it's ten dollars or ten thousand. We needed the money, and I found a way to provide it. You guys will be operating in the black because I could help, and instead of that being appreciated, I'm treated like I don't matter."

"I'll talk to Martin. He's got a lot of pride, and when Tony talked to the guy at the bank-" He sighed.

"I didn't want to insult anyone. I want to help. What Martin said, I guess it's the truth, I'm not a Ward."

"You're a Ward in every way that counts," he whispered, pressing his lips against her forehead. "I love you."

"I love you too." Natalie leaned into his embrace and shut her eyes as his hands moved over her back. "I'm going to grab a shower."

"We ordered out for dinner. I got you some of that chicken parm that you like."

"I don't want to go back downstairs."

"Don't hide in this room. This is your house, and Martin's gone by now. He left to find the next victim."

"I want to take a shower. I've got the early shift tomorrow, and I'm tired."

"Why don't I bring the food up here for you? We can watch television. I recorded reruns of Friends for you."

"Did you really?"

With a nod, he released her. "Go take your shower. I'll heat the food, and we can watch your show."

It was early that following morning when Martin returned home, and Natalie did her best to ignore him while she readied her coffee mug for the drive to work. He grunted as if not surprised and reached into the fridge, taking out the orange juice container to drink straight from the lid.

She turned to watch him take several gulps. "Do you not remember where the cups are located?"

"Of course I do. It's my house."

Natalie narrowed her eyes and snapped the lid of her tumbler on with a loud pop. "Look, I don't know what your problem is lately, but if you're not happy with me, you need to tell me about it because I'm sick of you being at my throat constantly."

He slowly lowered the carton. "I'm not trying to be at your throat, Tinkerbell." He paused to dig into his sweat pockets and pulled out her phone. "You left this in the bathroom. Some chick called about a donation for the hospital. Said she'd call you back later."

"Strange. They usually call human resources." She accepted the phone, "This isn't about the check. You've had a bad attitude for weeks. You may be miserable with your life, but that's not my fault."

"I am not miserable."

"Not even a little, Martin? Does it give you a warm fuzzy feeling to have a different woman in your bed every night? Do you like not having anything real when it comes to a relationship outside of your family?"

"You don't know what you're talking about, Nat. It must be that time of the month because you're being a real bitch right now."

"Calling me a bitch is inventive. I've never heard that before." Her words came out in a rush, even as she did feel like someone had punched her in the gut. "Not that it's any of your business, but it's not that time of the month for me. You're acting like an ass, and if you're not careful, you're going to end up with a painful burning sensation when you piss. I am not a bitch. If anything, I'm a damn doormat here, and I'll have you know that I've bent over backward since I've been here because I needed to show you all how much I appreciated everything that you've done for me."

Focused on him, she failed to notice Luke had come downstairs and stood in the kitchen doorway. "Martin, you're out of line."

"Please, stay out of this." Natalie looked over at him. "This has to happen. I'm already starting to feel uncomfortable living here, and I've only been moved in for two whole days."

"You said that you wanted to move in. You were here every night anyway."

"Maybe she's getting bored that she's not getting any action between the sheets, Little Brother."

"There's more to life than fucking, Martin. Maybe if you stopped to consider that, you wouldn't have women sneaking out of your bed in the wee hours of the morning."

"What the Hell is going on with you? You were never this bitchy when you were in my bed, Tinkerbell."

Natalie inhaled sharply, her mind reeling. She and Martin had become close very quickly. They might not have taken their relationship in any serious physical direction, but it was because she hadn't been able to let him in that way. In some ways, he'd always intimidated her. She'd never thought about what control it had taken him not to pressure her or seduce her into sleeping with him. He hadn't done either of those things because he cared about her. How much had it hurt when she'd ended things? No doubt he'd gotten over it in the year they'd been apart, but had it opened old wounds when she'd started to see Luke?

She was so lost in her thoughts that she didn't notice how Luke went stiff next to her. "You'd better apologize."

"I ain't apologizing for telling the truth," Martin responded with a cocky grin. It faded the moment Luke suddenly lunged forward.

Natalie watched in horror and fascination as the two brothers began to fight. It wasn't the playful wrestling she'd seen before. It was more like a bare-knuckle death match, and when they collided with the kitchen table, it made her jolt into action. Someone was bleeding. She couldn't tell who because there was blood on both of them and the floor that they were now rolling around. Panic flared, and she didn't know what to do. "Stop, please stop." She tugged at her hair as she heard Luke grunt. "Stop it!" Again, it was like they couldn't hear her.

She could not tell how much time had passed when she finally moved from where she was standing frozen. Determined to stop them once, she moved towards the sink. Turning the chilly water on full blast, she grabbed the sprayer and aimed. The water hit both men, and they cursed, sputtering as they finally moved away from each other.

"Natalie!" Luke sputtered, "That water is freezing! Cut it out!"

"The two of you cut it out!" She released the trigger but kept the sprayer firmly gripped in her hand. "Are you twelve? I asked you to stay out of it, Luke. Martin, you know what you said was completely inappropriate." Natalie sprayed the water a few more times. "But you've finally said something that makes me realize your problem, at least partly."

He glared at her and shoved wet hair back from his face. "What the hell are you talking about, Tinkerbell?"

"I'm sorry if the decisions that I've made have hurt your feelings somehow." She released the sprayer back into the sink and walked towards them. "You are a good man, Martin. You just weren't the man for me."

"Well, that's sweet, but you're taking things too personally," He grunted. "Ask anyone. I can be an asshole sometimes. You shouldn't be so worried about me." He flashed a quick smile. "I'm perfectly happy with the way that everything turned out."

She knew that he was lying, but there was little that she could say to make him tell the truth. She cleared her throat. "Maybe you should try to be less of an asshole."

He continued to smile. "Old habits are hard to break."

Days passed, and things returned to normal, or what resembled normal for the Ward family. Everyone fell into their daily routines, but Natalie noticed Martin stayed home more than usual. She didn't comment on it.

"You should have a whole bagel, not half."

"That half is for you." Natalie took another coffee mug from the cabinet when Luke entered the kitchen. "Are you sure that you should be going to work today?"

"I'm sure. Besides, Destiny needs help. Are you taking lunch?"

"They have chicken salad in the cafeteria today. I'll have that." She popped the last bite of bagel in her mouth. "I've got to go, or I'm going to be late."

"I'll text you." He leaned in to sneak a kiss.

"Take it easy today."

"Lukey always takes it easy, Tinkerbell." Martin strolled into the kitchen. He tossed her cell phone at her. "You forgot this upstairs."

With a roll of her eyes, Natalie swallowed the last of her coffee and easily caught the phone. "It's your turn for dinner, Martin. Let me guess, we're having pizza."

"How did you know?"

The rest of the morning passed in the blink of an eye. She forced herself to eat lunch and went down to the cafeteria, ordering a chicken salad sandwich and chips. She had taken a seat near the back when a shadow fell across the table, and she looked up to see Kimberly Carter, a high school friend whom she hadn't seen in years.

"Kimberly, this is a pleasant surprise."

The brunette smiled warmly, designer bag clutched to her side, as she briefly looked around. "I was in the neighborhood. I had no idea that you were a doctor here. That's great."

Natalie highly doubted Kimberly had any business at the hospital. Since her father passed away, she had thrown herself into running her family's business. She motioned across from her, and the woman immediately sat down. "I've worked here for a while but only recently became designated. How have you been?"

"Busy, but I can't complain. You?"

"Same." Natalie sipped her water and eyed Kimberly. "We haven't seen each other in years, Kimberly. You must have a reason for coming to the hospital. Is everything okay?"

"I had an interesting meeting today with a client named Anthony Ward. He brought his brothers, and I knew one of them."

Natalie paused with the bottle at her lips. "You had a meeting with Anthony Ward."

Kimberly nodded. "And his three brothers. I've been told you're currently dating one of them."

She lowered the bottle to the table. "And you're here because why exactly?"

"I might have hooked up with Martin at Ace's last night."

Natalie wanted to laugh at the look on the woman's face, but she withheld, cleared her throat, and paused to wipe her mouth with her napkin. "You slept with Martin?"

"It was... I don't know what it was," Kimberly sighed. "He wants to take me out on a date. I found out where you worked and figured I'd-"

"Dig for some information?" Natalie chuckled. "His attitude makes a lot of sense now. Martin's rough around the edges, but he's a good guy. I can't promise he's looking for anything serious, but he wouldn't purposely hurt you."

"I tried to end it with him today, but he doesn't take no for an answer."

"That he does not," she chuckled. "How did you find out I was dating Luke?"

"I might have had my secretary do a little digging. I tried to call your cell this morning instead of randomly showing up here, but Martin answered, and I panicked. I told him I was Melody and wanted to discuss a donation with you."

Natalie let out a delighted laugh. "That's so funny. He didn't suspect anything. He's clueless."

"I wouldn't go that far."

"Why would you say that?"

Kimberly's eyes opened widely as she focused on something over Natalie's shoulder. "Because he's here."

"What?" Natalie looked over her shoulder and cursed low under her breath. "This should be pleasant."

"Well, isn't this a coincidence?" With a wide smile, he grabbed a chair and pulled it over to the table. His eyes focused on Kimberly as he sat down. "Did you think I wouldn't recognize your voice on the phone?"

"I never assumed that you'd know my voice."

"What are you doing, Martin?" Natalie questioned.

"Don't start, Tinkerbell. The Princess and I are good friends." He didn't take his eyes off Kimberly. "Right, Princess?"

"Don't call me Princess."

He smirked. "So, how do you know Tinkerbell?"

"Kimberly and I went to Pittsburgh Arts Academy together."

"You went to private school?" His grin widened. "I should have guessed. I found this in the floorboard of my car after our meeting." He pulled a business card from his pocket. "You must have dropped it last night." He returned it to Kimberly with a wink. "So, what's for lunch?"

"I should go."

"Don't make me cause a scene. You know how I love those. I was hoping we could all have lunch together."

It amused Natalie that Martin and Kimberly could only focus on each other for the entire meal. They remained sitting there when she slipped away to go back to work.

The afternoon was more complicated than the morning, and she had to go to the ER and cover due to the department being short-handed. By the time she'd clocked out, she'd seen more blood and desperation than ever before. It was sobering, and she thought about how hard things had gotten for people in the area. She'd have to see if she could donate a little more each month to the local food bank or spend some time volunteering. She could even get Luke to agree to go along with her.

She debated the best way to approach him as she parked her car and walked into the house. She stopped at the scent of actual food cooking. "Martin, are you cooking? Destiny, you better not have taken his night again!"

"Destiny didn't take my fucking night," Martin announced, his voice coming from the kitchen. "Kimmy did."

Natalie stood in the doorway, an unmistakable look of shock on her face. She glanced between him and Kimberly standing at the stove.

"He might have talked me into it," Kimberly smiled softly.

Martin chuckled. "I talked you into a lot of things today." He leaned against the counter. "Do you want beer or wine, Princess?"

"I'll take a beer."

"Would you like one, Nat?"

Nodding, Natalie stepped into the kitchen, and he moved towards the fridge. So, what's on the menu?"

"I made meatloaf, mashed potatoes, and sweet corn."

"There's dessert, too." Martin handed them each a bottle of beer. He leaned in and captured Kimberly's lips for a quick kiss that made her blush. "I'm going to go check the score on the game; you okay in here?" She nodded and took a quick sip of her beer. He kissed her one more time with a wink. "Don't talk about me while I'm gone."

Natalie rolled her eyes and sipped her beer. "So, I guess you never made it back to the office today."

Kimberly blushed. "No, he managed to talk me into playing hooky."

She smirked with satisfaction. "He must have been very persuasive to get you to agree to cook, but Martin can be charming when he wants to be. He seems charmed by you."

"I don't know what we are, and I didn't mean to intrude on dinner. I can..."

"You can what, go?" Natalie shook her head. "I don't think so. You're not intruding on anything." She took another sip of her beer. "Is there anything I can do to help?"

"Everything is about done except for the meatloaf. That needs another ten or fifteen minutes. I set the table already."

"You set the table and cooked? Around here, the chef usually delegates stuff like that. You should keep that in mind."

"Uh, if you'll excuse me, I'm going to check my cell. I was waiting to hear back about a meeting my assistant was trying to set up." Kimberly shifted uncomfortably around Natalie and grabbed a sleek black purse from the hook on the wall. Natalie recognized the panicked expression in the woman's eyes. She'd had that same look when she first started falling for Luke.

Martin was going to have his hands full. Kimberly Ward was no stranger to the Pittsburgh tabloids. Her family was one of the first prominent ones to come out of the city. She had a family as controlling as her own. They had bonded over that in school.

Kimberly slipped out the front door onto the enclosed porch and smiled when Martin followed her. The door closed behind them, and beer in hand, she started up the stairs towards the room she shared with Luke. Had working worn him out so much that he'd needed to rest? The idea alarmed her, and she began to walk faster. She flung open the door and found him stretched out on the bed with an ice pack held against his forehead. "Oh God, what happened to you?"

"It's a scratch." He hissed as she yanked the ice pack away. "Fuck, come on."

"Oh, hold still, and let me see. How did you do this?"

"I don't want to talk about it."

"That's the wrong answer. How did this happen? You were supposed to go to the office and help Destiny catch up on paperwork! How do you get your forehead split open? Did you get into another fight with Martin?"

"Natalie, stop." Luke grabbed her flailing hands. "I need you to do something for me."

"What is it?"

"Kiss me, and I'll tell you what happened."

He would tell her anyway, and she wanted to kiss him, so she leaned in and let her lips brush against his. She pulled away with a smile before the caress could deepen. "What happened?"

"I was helping Destiny put boxes on the top shelf of the storage closet. I dropped one of the plastic records containers, and it bashed me in the head on the way down. Destiny almost twisted her ankle jumping out of the way."

"Poor baby." Natalie perched on the bed next to him. "You should have called me."

"I came back here to rest. That wasn't so successful. I put my earbuds on because Martin and his bimbo of the day were going at it like rabid rabbits."

"She's not a bimbo." She chuckled softly. "Her name is Kimberly, and besides Martin, she's probably the most stubborn person I've ever met."

"That sounds like a recipe for disaster." Luke grinned. "Did Destiny take pity on Martin and take his night? Something smells good."

"No, somehow he charmed her into doing it." She leaned over to kiss him again. "That's enough talking about them. That's enough talking in general."

Smiling, Luke grabbed and twisted her so her back was against the bed. He settled between her legs and buried his face against her neck. He rolled his hips against her and chuckled when she whimpered. "One thing is for certain; we're going to have to do something about the thin walls in this house." He nibbled on the curve of her neck.

"I can be quiet." Natalie slid her hand down to play with his belt buckle. He shifted away from her, and she pouted. "Come back here."

"No." He grinned widely and slid off the bed. He held his hand out to help her to her feet. "Soon, I promise."

"Now is better than soon." She pointed out with a slight whine to her voice. "Besides, I'm sure that Martin's now groping Kimberly on the porch."

"Well, we're going to interrupt them." Luke tugged her towards him. "I love you."

"I love you too, even if you're a horrible tease who should be ashamed of yourself!" She lectured playfully. "I'm going to make sure you pay for being a tease when the time comes."

"I look forward to it."

"Stop trying to create a perfect moment and realize that every moment with you is already perfect."

"Do you want to have this discussion again? You get mad, and while it's amusing, it's a vicious cycle."

"It's only vicious because there's no make-up sex involved."

Luke laughed and kissed her quickly before rushing down the stairs. He screamed his brother's name and pulled open the porch door. He tugged the door shut as quickly as he'd opened it. "We should give them a minute."

"Are they doing it?"

"They were..."

"Shut the fuck up, you two. Kimmy's shy. She's mortified right now."

"Mortified is a pretty big word for you, Martin. Do you need an ice pack or an aspirin?"

Luke questioned.

"Why don't you go jerk off?" Martin suggested. "Your balls have to be permanently blue now."

"Martin!" Kimberly exclaimed. "Don't fight with your brother like that."

"This is normal for them, Kimberly. I should have warned you," Natalie offered. "Come on, Luke, let's put the food onto the table and give these two a minute." She reached out for his hand and tugged him towards the kitchen. "Now tell me," She demanded in a harsh whisper. "What exactly were they doing?"

"I think Martin's right about Kimberly being embarrassed. I'm not going to say."

"Would I be embarrassed by it if I were the one who got busted?"

Chuckling, he draped his arm around her shoulders. "So, how do you know her?"

"Don't try and shift the conversation. You tell me everything anyway."

Luke paused. "Okay, fine. She was…"

"Who was what?" Warrick came through the back door with Destiny. "Why aren't there pizza boxes in the kitchen?"

"Martin's friend cooked actual food."

His eyebrows rose. "What friend?"

"By friend, do we mean a random hood rat?" Destiny asked with a sound somewhere between a scoff and a laugh. "Forgive me, but I don't want to get food poisoned by some random girl."

"She's not one of those girls," Natalie said quickly. "She's someone I've known for a while, and she's nice."

"Nice and Martin don't go together. If she's smart, she'll come to her senses and leave before she catches a disease."

"Destiny, you don't get it; he's sweet on her."

Warrick snorted. "It's more likely he's sweet on her head game."

Luke made a strangled sound somewhere between clearing his throat and a cough, a surprised sound that had Natalie's head turning towards him. "Is that it? Is that what they were doing?"

"I thought I told you two to shut up," Martin ordered as he came back in the house. "Rick, you're fucking late. You forgot to wipe your shoes off again and look at what you dragged into the house. Nice mustache, Cruella."

"I hope that your dick falls off, Martin."

"Rate he's going, it's likely to do just that," Warrick commented with a wide grin.

Martin rolled his eyes, flipping him off. "Watch your mouth."

Natalie caught sight of Kimberly in the hallway. The look on her face was enough to make her burst out laughing. She'd never seen the other woman so uncomfortable and unsure of herself. It was nice to know that even the Wards could Kimberly Carter sweat under pressure. "Why don't we all sit down and eat?"

"I'll start grabbing the stuff," Luke offered.

Martin shook his head. "You're whipped and not even getting any."

"Alright, that's enough," Natalie interjected. She suspected that Kimberly was about to flee in the opposite direction. She ignored Martin as he made a face at her. "Kimberly, will you help me with the drinks?"

"I was going to..."

Martin pushed his way into the hallway. "What were you going to do? I know that you're not leaving."

"I got a call from my assistant and..."

"Nice try, Princess, but your phone is right here." Martin slipped the phone from his pocket. "You really should pay more attention." He slid it back into his pocket. "You need to take a break from work and fucking relax."

"There's no need to swear."

"Don't act like me swearing offends you, Princess."

Warrick pushed forward past Natalie and Luke. "Why is she hiding in the hallway?"

"Guys..." Natalie's voice was lost in the conversation that followed.

Luke drew her to him. "Sit back and watch. It's more entertaining that way."

"It's not entertaining for her. You Wards can be an intimidating bunch."

"You're a Ward too, Natalie."

Even after the check fiasco, she felt like a family member, even though she knew some issues needed to be resolved with Martin. The man was being his usual hardheaded self, and while his sudden infatuation with Kimberly was a good sign, if he didn't deal with his unresolved issues, it wouldn't work. "I love you, Luke."

"I love you."

"Cut the mushy shit," Martin groaned. "You're ruining my appetite."

When she finally decided to call it a night, Natalie knew she'd regret the lateness when her twelve-hour shift loomed before her. She changed quickly, and Luke stripped down to the thermal long johns he had been hiding under his jeans. "Come on, you need to get some sleep for tomorrow."

"I'm not thinking about sleep."

"You never are," he tugged the covers back. "I like Kimmy. I'm unsure what she sees in Martin, but I liked her."

"He's very handsome and charming." She got into bed. He drew her close, and she shut her eyes as he wrapped his arms around her. "It's something that runs in the Ward family. Besides, he knows how to use his hands in ways that make you insane."

Luke groaned, "I don't need that mental image in my head."

"Replace it with something else." She shifted to face him. "Will it help if I say please?"

"You're trying to kill me. I'm in love with a sadist."

"Cut that out. You're the sadist; you're enjoying this. It isn't even hard for you."

"Trust me, it's hard. I want you never to forget the first time we're together."

"I'll never forget anything about you, Luke Ward."

She felt his lips press against her hair. "Will it make it easier for you if I tell you it will happen soon?"

"How soon is soon?" She shifted in his arms again. This time, she draped her leg over his in a provocative manner. "Is it five minutes from now?"

"It'd take me at least a half hour to undress you."

"That would drive me insane."

"That's the point."

Luke laughed. "You're not going to taunt me into making love to you." He stretched out and shut the light off. "You're going to be cursing up a storm in the morning when you've got to go to work."

With a growl, she shifted away from him. "Fine."

"Don't be like that."

"Be like what, Lukey?" She snuggled her face into the pillow to hide her smile. A laugh escaped her lips as he began to tickle her. "Cut it out!" She shifted to try and avoid him, and they began to wrestle playfully. "Luke Ward! I'm warning you." She choked the words out, trying desperately to suppress her laughter.

"It's bad when women laugh during sex, so you know." Martin's voice carried clearly through the wall from the hallway.

"Shut up. Martin!"

Natalie sighed and rested against the mattress. "I guess you've got a point about the walls being extra thin in this house."

Luke eased his weight down on her and raised his voice. "I think we'll need earplugs if Kimberly stays the night."

Martin pounded on the wall, and the hanging pictures rattled at the action. "At least I'm man enough not to care who hears me pleasing my woman."

"He called her his woman," Natalie whispered, eyebrows raised.

"Who'd have thought two Wards would fall for rich girls from the other side of the tracks." His smile faded at her blank expression. "What is it?"

"I'm not a rich girl. I know you all think that I am, but I'm not. That watch I pawned was the most valuable thing that I owned. I'll never see a dime from my parents." The fact didn't bother her as much as she'd feared that it would. It was only money. There were things entirely more important to her now than money, and she had all those things in bulk.

"Because you're with me."

"No, I knew all that was gone well before I met you." She'd never tell him he'd been the final nail in the coffin regarding her relationship with her family. Her mother had been horrified, and her father demanded that she come to her senses immediately. It was a conversation Luke knew nothing about, and she had no intention of telling him. "You're right, it's late, and we should sleep."

"Natalie, I love you more than anything in the world."

"That's good because that's how I love you."

Three Months Later

Natalie stood in the kitchen, wishing she could have slept ten minutes longer, but today was her day to make breakfast for everyone. She busied herself packing lunches for each of them. Soon, the house's quiet would be replaced with chaos, and she'd enjoy it as much as she enjoyed the time to herself and the soft ache between her legs. Luke hadn't lied when he said that soon they'd take their relationship further. It was like they couldn't keep their hands off one another. It was great. She loved every second of it.

Her life was damn near perfect. With Kimberly's offer of a renovation job, Ward Brothers Construction was operating in the black and showing a profit. Some would have called it nepotism had Kimberly not pulled entirely out of Martin's life shortly after the papers were signed.

Natalie didn't know why. The woman seemed so happy. Martin reacted to their breakup like it didn't matter, but she knew better. His actions told her that. He worked, ate, went to his room, and did it all again the next day. So, Natalie decided that the next time she saw Kimberly Carter, she was getting her ass kicked.

"Go back to bed, Tinkerbell. I'll finish up down here." Martin spoke from the doorway.

"I've got it handled. You're up earlier than I expected."

"I've got two guys out on the Mason renovation, and I need to keep an eye on it. I'm going to work a few extra hours tonight, so don't hold dinner for me." He moved forward to grab a coffee mug, and his eyes lit up with interest. "You're making pancakes?"

"If I had chocolate chips, I'd be making chocolate chip pancakes, but someone..." She sent him a sharp look because he'd been the one to do it. "Someone got the munchies and ate all the chocolate and peanut butter chips last night!"

"They tasted good together. You want me to run to the store for some?"

"No, we'll have regular pancakes. Everyone will live, I think." She smiled over at him. "You're starting to look like a caveman."

"Real funny, Tink."

"I wonder how many things there are living in your beard. Do you wash it with shampoo?" His new hair had been a constant source of teasing ammunition for the rest of the Wards. He responded in typical Martin fashion, swearing and threatening violence.

He shot her a humorless grin, but the expression slid from his face. He eyed the back door. "Who's in the backyard?"

She turned to see a woman with deep brown hair approaching the front door. "I don't recognize her."

"Go in the other room."

"I'm not scared of the girl in the Burberry coat." Natalie moved quickly to beat him to the door. "Hello, can I help you?"

"I'm looking for Martin Ward. Wait, is that you? You look like those cavemen in the car insurance commercials."

"Melody?" Martin frowned, or at least he did. It was hard to tell with the excess facial hair. "What are you doing here? Natalie, this is Melody, Kimberly's minion."

"I'm her assistant, thank you very much." Melody rolled her eyes. She was pretty, well dressed, and gave off the air of being a little eccentric. "And for the record, I was never here. You never saw me, and sadly, we never met, Natalie." Her eyes went back to Martin. "I was never here, got it?"

"All right, you were never here." Martin motioned for her to move inside the house. "Want a cup of coffee?"

"Yeah, thanks." Melody took off her black leather gloves and tucked them into her purse. "You should go and see Kimberly." She blurted out the words. "She's at the office, but she'll only be here tonight for the gala before she gets on a flight to New York."

"Why?" Natalie knew she was technically an outsider, but the question needed to be asked. "What's so important?"

"Look, I'm saying too much being here. Please, Martin."

"She doesn't want to see me."

"I love Kimberly, but her father did a number on her. She's emotionally fragile, even if she hides it well. You were getting to her, Martin. You were getting to her, and she couldn't take it, so she cut her losses and ran. You can't let her get away." The brunette turned her attention to Natalie. "You know her. You know how she is."

"She's a Carter. She's stubborn as a mule."

Melody smiled. "That's a good one. I will remember that and shamelessly pretend that I thought it up alone, but yes, she's bull-headed." She sighed. "Her entire life, it had been drilled into her that business comes first, and the company is what is most important. That was how her father lived, but that's not Kimberly."

"I can't just pick up and leave."

"Damn it, Martin, why not? You need to go after her!" Melody jumped up and down to emphasize the point. "If you don't go, you'll regret it for the rest of your life. You both will."

Natalie frowned. She eyed Melody and saw the desperation in her eyes. "I think you should go after her, Martin. Your brothers can handle the extra work."

"Thank you!" Melody threw up her hands in a dramatic gesture. "Go and shave that thing off your face so you don't get stopped for being suspicious. I need to go, but I'll tell you one thing: I'm tired of pretending I'm Kimberly. I'm not looking forward to doing it for the next few months when she goes to New York." She let her eyes meet Natalie's. "She'll be available only by phone conference if she gets on that plane."

"Listen to the woman, Martin. Why don't I get you a cup of coffee, Melody? We could chat."

"I really must go, but we should have lunch, and by do lunch, I mean eat at a fancy restaurant on Kimberly's dime because I can't tell you the last time I took time off. Hell, I violate the fire code daily to have a cigarette so that I don't snap someone's neck and the temp the agency sent me? Don't get me started." Melody pulled her gloves on. "Call me. Martin, give her the number before you leave." She glanced between them. "And remember, I was never here."

Martin's quick departure threw a wrench in work duties, and she called in sick to help with the extra paperwork. After staying home, she busied herself in the distracting work of stripping the wood floors like Luke had been supposed to do. It was grueling, dirty work, and she tried to liven it up by playing the radio loudly in the background. She sang along to the songs she liked as they played repeatedly. Memorizing the words hadn't even been something she'd wanted to do.

Once she fell into the rhythm, she let her mind wander back to Kimberly and Martin. The woman had been living there before they had a massive blowout. Would they still want to live there? Would they move to Kimberly's larger apartment?

Personally, Natalie couldn't picture them anywhere else but the Ward home. They could even turn one of the bedrooms into a nursery with some adjustments to the living arrangements. She and Luke could move to the apartment on top of the office. They hadn't rented it out because the Wards had trust issues. It would give everyone more space, and she didn't think Luke would object to them having some privacy.

Martin needed to hurry up and bring Kimmy back so that she could set a thousand plans flooding her mind into action.

She heard the front door slam and rose to her feet. "Hello?"

"It's me, Nat," Warrick called out. "I forgot my lunch." The thud of his work boots echoed through the house. "You got a lot done already. You're faster than Luke, but it's not hard to be."

"Luke works as hard as you do," she defended out of instinct. It was an issue for Natalie how hard he worked with his previous injuries. He should be more careful and spend more time at the office, but that would happen the day pigs fly.

"Whatever. Don't get your panties in a twist. I came to get my lunch." Warrick moved into the kitchen. "Hey, Martin's not here. I should take his lunch."

"I was going to take his lunch."

"Baby Girl, you don't like ham."

"I like it today." The sandwich had been on her mind all morning. "Take an apple or something if you're really that hungry."

"What the fuck is an apple going to do for me?" Warrick snorted with laughter.

"It'll give you vitamins and nutrients and keep the doctor away, meaning me when I stab you for taking that sandwich."

"Take it easy, Nat. There's no need to threaten violence. I'll leave the sandwich and take a damn apple." He stomped back into the living room and bit into the apple. "Damn, what crawled up your ass and grew claws?"

"You should have washed that apple first."

"A little pesticide never hurt anyone." He shrugged his shoulders. "I think I'll pick up some takeout on the way home."

"I want the Mexican place down the block. I want tacos and extra nachos with two sides of salsa, green, not red. Wait! Oh, half green and half red."

"I'll see what everyone else wants."

"I don't care. I want Mexican food. We're going to have Mexican." She stopped as if now hearing herself. "I'm sorry, Warrick. It was rude of me to make demands when you're offering to buy."

"Nah, it's cool. You should take a break and have lunch. Knowing you, you're cranky because you haven't eaten all day."

"Are you calling me cranky?"

"Hell, yes."

"Rick, go back to work and make yourself useful."

"Alright, crazy lady."

"Call me crazy again, and I will tell Destiny you're the one who ate the last donut yesterday." He said nothing else, laughing as he left the house. She lowered her tools and walked into the kitchen to wash her hands. She sighed and grabbed a magazine before sitting at the kitchen table.

She was feasting on her lunch and Martin's when Luke came through the back door with his lunch in hand. "Hey, Babe."

Natalie swallowed quickly. "Hey, I'm surprised to see you."

"The guys have busted their asses today, so I gave them an hour for lunch and figured I'd come home. Isn't there an extra lunch because Martin didn't take his?"

"I'm eating it. You can have half of my turkey on wheat if you're that hungry."

"You're eating his lunch and yours? Physical labor gave you one hell of an appetite today."

"Is the fact that I like to eat a problem? Like you've never had two sandwiches before." Natalie rolled her eyes. "I've seen you eat a whole pizza on your own!"

"I was saying you must be hungry. I never said there was anything wrong with it. I will take that turkey, though. I'm starving, too." He sat down across from her. "Now that Warrick and Destiny are gone, do you plan on telling me where Martin went?"

"That's Martin's story to tell." She eyed the pickle he unwrapped. She'd forgotten she'd given him the last pickle. "I want that pickle."

"What?"

"I want that pickle," Natalie repeated. "It's the last one. I was trying to be nice when I gave it to you, but now, I want it."

"We could split it."

"Fine, keep your stupid pickle."

"What the... Have you been inhaling the fumes from the solvent you're using?"

"I have not been huffing anything, thank you very much. I'll get my own pickle, a whole jar of pickles!" She grabbed the other half of the sandwich. "Asshole." She added for good measure.

"Babe, you can have the pickle." Luke extended it to her. "I didn't think that you wanted it that badly."

"I don't want now."

His mouth dropped open. "What has gotten into you? It's a pickle."

She took another bite of the sandwich and eyed the roast beef and Swiss cheese in his hand. Damn it, why did it look so good? Luke stared at her as if she had two heads. "Are you going to eat your whole sandwich?"

"Uh, no." He cleared his throat and handed her half. He placed the pickle on her plate as well. "Here you go, Baby."

"Thanks. This is so good for some reason. I'm starving."

"I'm confused. You hate roast beef. You won't even touch it to make the sandwich." He pointed out.

"I decided I wanted to try it. Is that a crime?"

"Of course not, it's ... Well, it's surprising because you don't usually try things that you don't like. Are you okay?"

"I'm fine. Why? Do I look sick? Do I look bad? Is it my hair?"

"Baby, you're beautiful." He said without hesitation. "You're acting a little differently."

"I am not." She paused and looked down at the items crowded on her plate. It was loaded, and she still wanted the pickle even though she wouldn't admit it. "Okay, so I'm a little cranky today. I can't be Miss Sunshine every day of my life."

"And no one expects you to be. Tell me what's going on?"

"Nothing is going on. It's a rough day."

"Honey, it's not today. These past few weeks... I'm concerned. The thought crossed my mind that it's a hormone thing."

"If you say anything about it being that time of the month, I may maim you with a common household item."

"See, that's what I mean? That was... Well, it was a pretty gross mental image." He cleared his throat. "That wasn't the type of hormone I had in mind. I wondered if you might be pregnant."

"I can't be pregnant. You're the one who puts on the condom every time we're together."

"They're not always a hundred percent effective."

"We're careful, Luke. It's a ridiculous idea." Natalie scoffed and reached to snatch the pickle. "What?"

"I want you to take a test. Destiny has some upstairs in the bathroom, and I'm sure she wouldn't mind if we borrowed one."

"Borrowed it? We'd use it and give it back? That's pretty gross if you ask me." She bit into the pickle and sighed. "This is better than I thought it would be. It may be better than sex. Sorry, no offense, but it's true right now."

"I'm going upstairs to get the test. Guzzle some water."

"Luke, I'm not pregnant." Her words were met with deaf ears. She sighed. Now that he mentioned it, she did have to pee. She'd point out to him how wasteful it was to use a test that cost ten dollars.

He came bounding back into the kitchen. "Here we go. Come on, we'll use the bathroom down here."

"Luke, the ten dollars that test costs will give me enough gas to return to work for a week. We might be getting more income from Four Brothers Construction now, but it's in our best interest to be as careful as possible."

"We're taking the test, Natalie. Please, do it for me."

"Fine, I'll piss on a stick, but you'll see I'm not pregnant. It's sweet that you're so anxious and excited, Luke, but we both know now is not the right time. We're not ready."

She repeated those exact words three minutes later when the evidence of the test was in front of her. There was no denying it. "It doesn't matter if we're ready, Natalie, we're going to have a baby. Oh God, we're going to have a baby." His excitement was undeniable.

It was also contagious, and she found herself smiling. Suddenly, there was nothing else she could think of but the fact that life blossomed inside her. How had she not realized it? How had she not seen the signs?

"We've got to call everyone and tell them."

"Why don't we wait? It's still early. There could be complications."

"If there are, we'll deal with them as a family. Everyone is going to be so happy."

"I ..."

"I know that you're scared. I'm scared, too, but we'll figure it out. I promise."

"This is so unexpected," Natalie sighed. "What if we suck at it?"

"I can promise you we won't suck at it. Do you believe me?"

"You've never lied to me."

"I never will, Natalie, not ever. Let's share this happy news with our family."

Piper lives in Tennessee with her husband, two children, and their dog, Denver. She enjoys writing, reading, and horror movies. She aims to retire on vast acres of land in the middle of nowhere. Follow her on Facebook, TikTok, and Instagram.

Made in the USA
Coppell, TX
04 December 2023

25280885R10100